AN ARCANIST PROBLEM IN RENO

THE PHOENIX DRC

KEVIN A DAVIS

*For April
Always April.
She endures my obsession with my characters, wild rants, and me
working seven days a week.*

*In Memory of David Farland.
A guiding teacher who was always passionate about mentorship and
writing. You are loved and missed.*

AN ARCANIST PROBLEM IN RENO

CONTENTS

Introduction	ix
Also by Kevin A Davis	xi
Chapter 1	1
Chapter 2	5
Chapter 3	14
Chapter 4	22
Chapter 5	26
Chapter 6	34
Chapter 7	40
Chapter 8	52
Chapter 9	59
Chapter 10	66
Chapter 11	75
Chapter 12	83
Chapter 13	89
Chapter 14	97
Chapter 15	104
Chapter 16	112
Chapter 17	119
Chapter 18	127
Chapter 19	133
Chapter 20	140
Chapter 21	147
Chapter 22	154
Chapter 23	160
Chapter 24	167
Chapter 25	175
Chapter 26	183
Chapter 27	192
Chapter 28	200
Chapter 29	206

Chapter 30   212
Chapter 31   219
Chapter 32   222
Chapter 33   225
Chapter 34   229

Afterword   233
Consociation Records   235
Acknowledgments   275

INTRODUCTION

If you've read the DRC Files, then some of these characters have been introduced. They are a large reason I splintered off to Phoenix. I loved their personalities, and wanted more.

Zach Graves has been rambling about in my head as a modern man not tangled up in the patriarchy with ego and machismo. Able to listen and ready to jump in, he starts off in a terrible place, but I plan better times for him.

I hope you enjoy Zach and the Phoenix DRC as much as I do.

Also by Kevin A Davis

If you'd like to be kept up to date on this series or my other books, please head to my website and join my mailing list

The DRC Files - an episodic paranormal procedural with Kristen Winters and the DRC team out of Atlanta

The Phoenix DRC - a spinoff of the award-winning DRC Files where Zach Graves joins the team headquartered in Phoenix, Arizona

The Khimmer Chronicles - the spunky Ahnjii makes new friends and enemies while stranded on a cryptic-filled earth

The Sorrowborn Trilogy - a YA Adventure Romance by April Davis & Kevin A Davis featuring the indomitable Caitlyn

The AngelSong Series - Haddie deals with ancestral powers in this gritty series of angels, demons, and fallen angels

Website KevinArthurDavis.com

Facebook @KevinArthurDavis

KevinADavis on Instagram

KevinADavisUF on Twitter

ONE

Zach Graves studied the large blue tent at the back of the site under spotty shade. *Tent is going to be an oven,* he thought. The coffeepot sat on the wooden picnic table, while the cooler waited pinned under the bench.

Zach wiped the back of his neck with a towel, beaming at Beth through a dark stubble that spread from his short black hair. He'd let it grow out a little more than usual. "Damn good start to the trip, don't you think?"

Her brown hair unkempt from the swim, she eased the van into the campsite, eyes focused ahead of them. "This is all you, babs. I'm not big on sweating." Her tattoos rippled as she put the vehicle in park.

From the back, Peter leaned between their seats, his wet blond hair neat and in place. "You like making 'em sweat, though, in the courtroom."

With a wink, Zach clasped Peter's hand on his chair back, and locked his gaze with blue eyes. "Oh, that's right. Didn't someone just win an important case?"

"Me!" Beth smiled. "Incorrigible flirts." She unbuckled, then opened the driver's door and hopped down. "I need to change out of this suit."

The side sliding door ground open as Peter exited, while Zach grabbed his and Beth's water bottles, letting them clang dully against each other and the keys to his van. The Arizona summer air had a spicy, mesquite odor even this high in the mountains. "I'm pulling the hammocks," he said as he exited.

Peter followed Beth to the tent, waving over his head. "Don't forget my pack. My cheese is still in there."

Zach huffed, loud enough to hear, but grinned as he moved to the rear doors of his old white Ford van. The hinges groaned, and among the guitar stands and toolbox, he pulled out the bagged hammocks by their cords from under the back bench.

Beth cried out, a light chirp of surprise.

When Peter yelled and cursed, Zach dropped everything in the sand to whip around the doors. The tent jostled, threatening to topple from whatever had startled the others. *Snake? Spider?*

With a tightness in his chest, Zach broke into a run before something unnatural growled. He managed one more stride before Peter's voice cut off and dark liquid sprayed the side of the blue tent.

Beth chanted what might have been, "No, no, no," before her body flew out of the opening to the tent.

As she skidded on her back into the sand, her hands grasped at the ruins of her neck where blood gushed onto the ground. Her brown eyes peered toward the tent, fluttering and never seeing him arrive.

A gray shape loomed inside, then turned, shambling out of sight.

Peter.

Zach stumbled over Beth's body, ripping aside the flap.

A ghoul, a resident of the Tarus realm, had its back turned to him. Peter's corpse sprawled across their sleeping bags with his neck torn out as well. Blood coated one side of the tent and soaked into their bright bed. The ghoul, a flesh eater, ignored Zach and moved to feast on Peter's body.

A scream from somewhere deep in Zach filled the tent, forcing the cryptid to spin and face him. The hot air reeked of blood, a metallic odor. A fouler, rancid scent wafted from the creature.

The mindless cousin of vampires, the ghoul had wet, black eyes that appeared all pupil. Its long black claws dripped blood and flesh. The body and head could have been a gray-skinned human, but it lacked hair, genitals, or anything that might have indicated birth, birthing, or life. Sharp gray teeth crowned a mouth with no lips or tongue.

With a step backward into the flaps, Zach dug into the Dur-Alf realm, pulling out a binding spell. His pulse pounded, not with fear for his own life, but with rage.

The ghoul charged, pulling back a too-long arm for a clawed strike, and Zach moved forward.

A more intelligent cryptid might have adjusted, but a ghoul possessed only insatiable hunger.

Zach slammed his binding spell, his palm, and all of his tall frame's muscle into the smooth, gray chest of the monster. His rage bellowed as he struck, and the spell took, locking the cryptid into place. The sheer force of the impact stopped the ghoul's momentum and sent it toppling back onto the floor of the tent.

Silence echoed in Zach's ears as he stared down at the ghoul, arm stretched for a strike, lying trapped and rigid beside Peter's mutilated corpse.

"Peter," Zach whispered. *How?* His seething anger swelled like a volcanic maelstrom rising to the surface, and he pulled another spell from the moss-green realm of Dur-Alf. His mother had trained him on the crushing spell, but he'd never needed it in life; it came awkwardly.

Heavy and draining, he lifted it with his right hand and slammed it down atop the ghoul. The ground shook as the magic activated, grinding an impossible weight against the cryptid. Bones snapped, flesh flattened, and dark blood spurted out in every direction.

Zach dropped to his knees.

CHAPTER

TWO

When the park ranger arrived, I lay at Beth's side, my head resting on her abdomen, unable to look at what remained of her throat or blood-splattered face.

The stench of the ghoul made my stomach churn. A gaggle of onlookers had gathered, murmuring and gasping, but no one had dared approach me. My mind sputtered, trying to make sense of this. Neither Beth nor Peter was a witch, so someone had set a ward to open Tarus, letting in the closest of the nightmare denizens. *Who?*

"Holy shit!" a young woman exclaimed. Then, her voice turned hard with authority. "Don't move."

I lay in my swimming trunks and remained with my temple and cheek against Beth's soft flesh. It had cooled by a degree or two.

"Get up."

Make up your mind. The true authority, the Department of Realm Containment, would arrive at some point, and until then, the park service and police would want to control me.

"Hands over your head."

I shifted slowly, noting her nervous shuffle. *Did I care if she shot me?* Eyes closed, I sat and placed my palms on my damp hair.

"Knees," she said. "On your knees."

I opened my eyes, not letting them drift up Beth's body to the torn flesh, though I would remember the sight of her shredded neck forever. With slow shifts, I got one calf and heel under me, then the second. My focus locked on the stake in the ground that held the white cord tethered to our tent.

Red Aegis, I thought, my mind sharpening in the new position. I'd sent the query out just the day before. No one else would have a reason to attack me. *This had been meant for me.* I winced as a pain, like a long, sharp needle, stabbed into my chest. *My fault.*

The ranger asked me what happened, and I ignored the question. I couldn't answer. Even if I didn't work for the Consociation, I knew better than to involve mundanes.

Voices murmured like ghosts around us. The police arrived with a new set of commands and demands. Memories replayed of Peter and Beth entering the tent.

"Zachary Graves?" an officer asked. I didn't answer, and they dug through the scene, yelling at onlookers.

After a while, a heat-flushed officer clamped cuffs on my wrists, though my fog kept the surrounding bedlam to a distant buzz. I walked when the police told me to and folded myself into the rear seat of their cruiser. The rancid odor of stale vomit recycled through the air conditioning.

"Who is the corpse?" the red-faced officer demanded from the open door.

Beth. Peter. The other remains you wouldn't understand, I thought. A vague memory of their names being mentioned by an officer trickled past the veil between me and the horror of reality. As my eyes closed, Beth and Peter's parents loomed in the darkness of my mind. The police would notify them.

The rough shove on my shoulder brought my rage to the surface, and I spun in my seat to glare at the officer. Overfed and flabby, he staggered a step back, hand darting to his weapon. I could have the cuffs off with an unlocking spell, and follow with a binding, but he wasn't my enemy. His eyes were wide as he retreated and swung the door shut.

I sagged, resting my head against the metal grate between me and the driver's seat. The rumble of the engine and the whispering air conditioner muffled the outside world.

An officer barked nearby, and I lifted my head.

One onlooker, a sharp-faced man with jet-black hair and mustache, stopped his approach to the cruiser that held me. He wore a gray sports jacket and white shirt with no tie, and his sweaty, pale skin proved him to be over-dressed for the weather outside. The man forced a smile and said something inaudible as he retreated to the bright tape where the other onlookers waited. Likely a reporter, he'd have a hard time keeping a story once the DRC showed up.

I returned my gaze to my bare feet. How had the Red Aegis found out that I'd sent a query about their ISP via the FBI? The trail had been difficult since the moment I'd gotten the lead from a DRC agent, Kristen Winters. Following up with her had been less than illuminating, as everything had been in her report.

After three days of digging, I'd found the connection on a Discord channel between Russell Howard and a person named Melchor, who had given him the download link for the ritual. Melchor, hopefully from the Red Aegis, had deleted their messages, but I'd retrieved them.

The ISP must have responded with a name for the owner of the website. A name I wanted now more than ever.

My identity wouldn't have been sent to the ISP. I'd gone through one of the Consociation connections in the FBI's cybersecurity division. The leak had to be there. I'd get the name of the website owner on Monday, and a list of the agents in my FBI contact's division. *That's where I'll start.*

I winced at the sharp malice that clung to the thought. *Vigilante justice or investigation?*

The FBI showed up in less than an hour and transferred me to one of their SUVs without berating me with questions. Standard procedure for the DRC. Federal employees were easier to silence than state or local.

The local police had already examined and placed Beth into a body bag, which they left under the jurisdiction of jacketed FBI. Through the tinted window, I stared at her form. My thoughts recycled around the Red Aegis, Russell Howard, and a mole within the FBI who had doxed me.

When the door opened, I suppressed a flinch and raised my head.

"Zachary Graves?" The agent, dressed as FBI, had bright pink hair that worked nicely with their dark suit. The voice and fit of the black jacket led me to assume them nonbinary.

When I didn't answer, they gestured for me to exit. "Do you prefer Zach?"

"Yes," I said wearily.

I studied the three of them, running through reports in my mind. The local DRC was out of Phoenix. The five-foot-six pink-haired one would be Mika, a Merfolk. *Team leader.*

A redheaded agent unlocked my cuffs with keys while the realm of Ya Keya bloomed about her. *Dagen. Werewolf.* She sniffed audibly. With a solid build, she brimmed with energy and had the air of a scrapper ready to find a brawl at the local bar.

Quiet and observant, a woman with long brown hair stood motionless. *Olivia. Vampire.* The third member of their team studied me from a distance with dark, sharp eyes that flicked from my face to my hands as I rubbed at the red grooves left in my wrists.

"You work in the SDS, correct?" asked Mika.

I nodded. They had a full report on me by now. The Subversion and Delinquency Surveillance Division did not like to share directly with other Consociation departments, preferring to run everything through the Executive Committee. It would take a while before this group would get details about my previous week's activities, but they probably already knew my workout schedule and streaming preferences.

"What happened?" Mika asked.

"They went in the tent. A ghoul attacked them. I killed it."

"Where did the ghoul come from?"

If I told them about my investigation of the Red Aegis, I'd be breaking protocol. Besides, I didn't want them interfering. "Inside the tent. How it got there, I do not know." I glanced at Olivia, who watched me with disturbing intensity and without blinking.

Dagen had moved away and paced about the site behind the tent.

"What is your theory?" Mika's expression never

changed, remaining somewhere between affable, curious, and serious.

"Someone wanted me dead."

The redheaded werewolf huffed. "No shit."

Mika shifted, as if to silence or chastise, but stopped to glance at Olivia, who spoke in a straightforward manner with no emotion. "Is it related to your work with the SDS?"

I unclenched my teeth. "Someone, attempting to kill me, killed two people that I love very much. I'm trying to work with you, but my patience is thin."

"As is mine." Mika cocked their head, with no hint of humor in their expression.

"What do you expect of me?" I asked, barely controlling my tone.

With a flicker of a false smile, Mika turned. "Could you grab us some waters?"

Olivia's eyes trailed mine, even as she moved to comply.

I followed as Mika gestured to the picnic bench, and we took a seat. "I'm sorry for your loss."

My mood already shattered and dark, I didn't respond.

As I sat, a jingling stretcher caught my attention. A tall, pale woman with bound yellow hair ignored us, intent and focused as she rolled toward the tent. *Another member of their team.*

"Yasmine?" I asked Mika. I often got well-detailed coroner and forensic reports from someone of that name who worked with their team.

"Yes, she'll be quick and have the bodies ready for a funeral."

Funeral. The faces of our friends and family flashed as I blinked. I leaned my elbows against the rough wood and buried my face in my hands, letting the parade of loved ones float against the darkness.

"We tried to recruit you. I believe it was in 2016."

I lifted my face and studied her. "What does that have to do with . . ." My voice faltered, rising in pitch. Guilt stabbed my chest. I wouldn't have been working on the Red Aegis.

Mika shrugged, bobbing their head to one side. "Nothing at all."

Olivia stepped toward us, footsteps light as she carried two waters. She locked eyes with mine, but said nothing as she handed me a bottle.

"Where's mine?" asked Dagen from behind me.

With a casual lift of their chin, Mika indicated the SUV where Olivia had retrieved the water bottles. "Right where you left it."

Dagen scoffed, stomping past us. "One male scent. Human."

I straightened, conscious that Mika and Olivia studied me, but asked, "Peter, or someone else?"

Mika shook their head, denying me any facts.

My eyes tightened. They hoped to squeeze the information about the Red Aegis from me with a carrot. I remained silent, loosening the cap and drinking.

At the tent, Yasmine called. "Mika."

With my back to the dwarf, I refused to turn as Mika rose, pointing at me to remain at the table. My throat tightened as I guzzled the water, but I didn't show my frustration. Muffled voices sounded from inside the tent, and I stared at the distant band of bright ribbon where the FBI kept a pair of camera-wielding journalists at bay.

Dagen returned and took Mika's seat. She took a sip of her water. "So, where were you before you came back to the site?"

"Swimming, hiking." *The vacation we were supposed to enjoy.* Frustrated, I couldn't hear what Mika and Yasmine discussed, but buried my anger.

"Explains the outfits. The swimming part."

"What more do you need from me?" I asked. The Consociation would expect me to help without divulging my department's activities, but this disconcerted questioning needled me.

"Can you exclude all of your recent work activities from involvement in this case?" asked Olivia.

"Case?" I asked. My legs tensed, but I kept from rising.

Olivia nodded in concession. "A bad choice of wording, but my question stands."

Before I snapped at them, I replaced the cap on my empty bottle and set it on the table. I steepled my fingers in front of me, focusing on the distant reporters as I answered. "Any of my activities in the past month could be reason enough to attack me. As you well know, the work I do might bring retaliation from arcanists or witches, any of whom might have the ability to leave a ward to Tarus." I sickened slightly, reliving the nightmare. What I needed was a good run to clear my head.

I dropped my chin to my fingers, scratching the light fuzz across the tips as I continued, "You are also aware that I cannot divulge any of those investigations without explicit directives. It is against protocol."

Dagen slammed down her water. "You'd just let someone get away with this?"

Mika spoke at my shoulder. "Of course he wouldn't."

My shoulders stiffened, but I maintained my position, fingers to my chin, breathing calmly despite the maelstrom inside.

Olivia shifted her focus from me to Mika. "You believe he'll attempt his own vengeance?"

"I believe that we need to gather some clothes for Zach and bring him back to the office where we can discuss this further without distractions. The FBI will retrieve everything they can and return it to the office with the van, but that might be much later tonight. In the meantime, we'll make some calls to see if we can get Zach released to speak with us." Mika clapped my shoulder, sparking the blue of Mer at my side. "What do you say?"

I shut my eyes. I would endure this. The SDS moved slowly, unless the executive committee got involved. My office wouldn't be open until Monday, tomorrow, then I could prudently retrieve the information and be on my way. Until then, Mika would watch to see if I did anything outside of the usual. *Like sneak into my office today when it's closed.*

"What choice do I have?" I asked rhetorically.

Dressed in the sweaty shorts and T-shirt that I'd hiked in earlier, I slid into the backseat with Dagen. My wallet, keys, and phone hadn't been retrieved. Olivia started the engine as Mika took the passenger seat.

"Aren't there four of you?" I asked.

Red-haired Dagen glared at me as if she might rip my head off. She yanked at her seatbelt without a word.

Mika twisted in the front to face me. "We lost Phistrel last week." They studied my unsure reactions and clarified. "We just had his funeral."

"On the job?" I knew it happened among the DRC teams, just not often.

"Yes."

The SUV crept into motion, and the FBI made space for us to exit onto the campground road. I leaned back in my seat and studied the onlookers, mostly reporters. I'd gotten the initial report on the mention of the Red Aegis last weekend, flagged to my desk as priority. The suspect, or victim, had been in Montana, though the agent worked out of Atlanta. *So, a joint effort?*

Phistrel had died on the same case.

Mika spoke softly on the phone in the front while Dagen slouched with a scowl, leaving me to watch out my window in silence. We'd arrive in Phoenix in the afternoon, but Mika probably already worked on getting authorization to my cases. If, as I hoped, the SDS kicked it up to the executive committee, I should have about twenty-four hours before the team had access to the Red Aegis files. I'd be in and out of my office by then, if my FBI contact had gotten Melchor's identity. *If not?* I frowned.

Between phone calls, Mika had attempted to interact with me with idle chatter, but I'd answered with terse, one-word answers. Then she pressed too close to the gaping wound that the ghoul had left in my heart. "Is there anyone you need to contact?

"Can you just—" My mouth snapped shut, and I balled my fists at my side, glaring at her. We still had an hour before we reached Phoenix, and they continued the interrogation. My life lay in ruins, and I held onto one last thread, Melchor's identity. I calmed my tone. "Sorry. I'm just trying to process all this."

When we dropped out of the mountains and Olivia pulled into a gas station, my mood had descended into a bitter state. I couldn't get the images of Beth and Peter out of my mind, and the wait to find their killer had me grinding my teeth.

"Hungry?" Mika asked.

My queasy stomach roiled at the thought. "Not hungry." In the still, summer heat, the sharp scent of gas hung at the pumps, and I headed for the store, more to get away from them than anything else. The bathroom stank so foul that I thought I might retch.

Dagen, with a scowl, and inquisitive Olivia watched me as I wound my way toward the front. Mika finished with a woman at the register and dug in a bag before intercepting me at the door. "Kombucha?"

Spite flushed hot on my cheeks; they'd dredged so deep into my profile they knew what I liked to drink. Instead of snapping out a biting remark, I took the bottle. "Thanks." I'd have to be very careful with this team.

"I know this is tough," Mika said as I held open the door.

You have no idea. In silence, I returned to my seat.

In the afternoon traffic, we exited the highway, heading east. The FBI building near my Consociation office housed the DRC. I knew that much. On the way to work during the week, I passed the fenced-in complex and never thought about it.

We pulled through a secured gate and drove into a dark garage that felt like a tomb. I wanted to resent them for wasting my time, but all that awaited me was a small house packed full of tortuous memories. If I were honest, I didn't relish going home.

Mika swept me past security in a manner that told me it grated against protocol, but the guard only watched with tight lips. "We're right here on the ground floor." A pair of jacketed agents waited at an elevator farther down a sterile hall. Mika stopped at the first door on the right, plain gray with "DRC" lettered on a plaque. The wall stretched a good distance before another door broke the monotony.

Big, I thought. My cubicle at the SDS measured twelve feet at the widest.

Mika keyed a pad, and the door clicked open. I followed into a hall five yards deep, wondering about the three doors at the end. Under dull lights, our footsteps echoed in the tight confines.

We entered the door on the left, stepping into a large room. "Welcome to the Pit," Mika said.

Straight across the room waited another door, possibly a closet. On the wall to my right was a whiteboard with an eight-foot conference table set far enough away that a chair could fit. Along the sides of the rest of the room were four desks with monitors and high-backed office chairs. Mika patted the tabletop, walking to one of the middle desks.

Dagen bristled beside me as Mika rolled a chair toward me before heading to the far side for another. *Four chairs.* One had belonged to Phistrel. *The team's office.*

Olivia wasted no time collecting what I assumed was hers from a neatly organized desk with two monitors. Dagen stomped back with another from the corner.

Mika dropped into their chair, kicking off the desk to roll to the conference table. "Sit."

I took the offered seat with reluctance. "How long is this going to take?"

"Do you have something planned?" Mika cocked their head.

Olivia placed her chair at the table, then headed for the door, disappearing back into the hall. I watched her exit without responding to Mika's bait.

Dagen sat, promptly kicking her heels up to the table six inches from where my arm rested.

"If—" Mika paused and smiled "—I were working on a case that got my partners killed, I would have a plan in place to bring them justice." The emphasis on the last word hung in the air over the table. In the pause that followed, a door clicked out in the hall, close enough that it had to be one of the three. "The guilt would drive me to act on emotion, rather than logic."

My face flushed, but I didn't react.

"Justice," Mika stated. "An odd word since it depends upon context, bias, and cultural values."

"And law," I said, regretting it, but following through to close the implication. "For whoever killed Beth and Peter. Whether or not it's revenge for some past investigation of mine."

"Consociation law." Mika eased back in their chair. "My people would have a different view, in a case such as yours. If we were a human entity, such as the FBI—" with a dismissive wave they gestured to the ceiling "—we would handle the situation with other protocols based on their traditional values."

I didn't disagree, but grasped for Mika's manipulation in all of this. As the door in the hall clicked, I refrained from replying, content to let them ramble.

Dagen rocked in her chair as Olivia returned only as far as the doorway, speaking in the silence. "I'm going up front to wait."

"Thank you." Mika offered a genuine smile, waited for the door to close behind Olivia, and leaned onto the table. "As I said earlier, if my actions inadvertently led someone to harm those I loved, I'd want justice. Aligned, of course, with the dictates and law of the Consociation." Then, the dialog twisted. "Your mother, Samantha Graves, works in the ISL department. Interspecies liaison. Is that correct?"

Is this an attempt to shame me into complying? I force my face to relax. "Yes."

"Your father, Jim, does not work for the Consociation, though he is a witch." Mika did not appear to need me to answer, but took a moment. "It is as you likely expected."

The last comment confused me. "What is?"

"The SDS has referred our request for your case files to the executive committee. They have also reminded me personally that it would be against protocol for you to divulge said information without their express permission."

Dagen swore, kicking her shoes down and standing up to pace.

I sighed and leaned forward. "What am I doing here, then?"

"We are currently investigating a serious case, as you know. Did you see the sigil in the tent?"

"No." I hadn't even looked. My thoughts flashed back to Yasmine calling Mika into the tent.

"Rather unique in form and delivery. I wondered why you hadn't mentioned it."

Without a thought, I wet my lips. "In what way?"

Mika shrugged. "Not really my place to say."

With a deep breath, I settled my burst of frustration. "Can I leave yet?" I asked. The DRC had no intention of feeding me information, as I would not help them.

"I have more questions."

The door opened, surprising me enough that my head snapped to Olivia, who entered with three plastic bags. Mika stood to help.

I recognized the sushi containers from one of my favorite restaurants. My temper almost won, but instead, I leaned on the table, steepling my fingers. Mika had made their point. "Obviously, you have considerable resources in the DRC. Far superior to anything I could manage when it comes to dealing out justice." I left the hint of sarcasm in the last word. "You said you had more questions."

"After we eat." Mika slid a container toward me, no doubt with one or more of my favorites inside.

"I'll wait." My heart sank, realizing I didn't necessarily want to go to my house. I considered my parents, or William from the band, but couldn't bear either idea.

Mika ignored my refusal to open the container and sat

with a large order and chopsticks. When their phone rang, they listened for a moment before answering, "Yes."

Dagen picked up her order and ate while standing. Olivia had nothing, but placed a bottle of iced green tea in front of me.

The door outside closed, then ours opened. A gray-haired woman with a streak of lavender stormed into the room, heading directly for Mika. Dressed in jeans and a Darth Vader T-shirt, she moved spryly for someone in their fifties or sixties. Her expression tightened as she appraised me and the rest of the team. *As sharp as Mika and Olivia*, I thought. She held my phone and placed it on the table, but not in front of me. "Neddie Harris. Data and communications." Her introduction, clipped and sharp, surprised me as I'd half expected her to ignore me.

I picked up the iced tea, popped the cap, and nodded. "Zach Graves, but you likely know that."

"Of course, but it is only polite." Neddie studied each of the members of the DRC, shook her head, and marched back out, slamming the door behind herself.

As I took a sip of the tea, Mika tossed my phone with a sharp, too-fast move. It soared straight across the table with a trajectory that would send it close to my drink before crashing into the wall. Left-handed, I snatched it out of the air without spilling the bottle in my right.

"Nice catch."

"Oh, crap!" shouted Dagen. "Hell, no."

At a flick of Mika's finger, Olivia placed my wallet and keys on the table beside my untouched food.

I frowned at Dagen, trying to unravel her reaction. She just glared at me like I'd run over her dog and she wanted to place me under a wheel.

"I checked," said Mika, procuring another piece of sushi with the chopsticks, "it was 2016."

Dagen swore in a near growl.

It took me a long moment to recall a previous comment. "The recruitment offer?"

"Why did you reject it?" Mika popped the sushi in their mouth.

Because Mom would kill me. She hadn't approved of my joining the SDS. "I wasn't interested."

The emotions, guilt, and trauma had muddled my thinking, but it became clearer as I juggled pieces of the conversation together. They had shown me their efficiency by digging into my personal file. The Red Aegis would be exposed to them, possibly with Melchor's identity. After that, they'd be only a step behind me. Mika's trying to recruit me.

I straightened, putting down my drink. "No." With a glance at Dagen, obviously mourning her teammate, I emphasized my refusal. "Under no circumstances will I join the DRC."

CHAPTER

FOUR

When I climbed into Olivia's tiny convertible Porsche, my shins scraped on the glove box. The odor of hot plastic permeated the inside. Even sheltered in the garage, the temperature ranged well over a hundred.

"You live close," Olivia observed. She clicked her seatbelt and started the little car, leaving the roof up as the air conditioning whirred under the dash.

I saw no point in answering. I'd rejected Mika's offer to join the DRC for a grueling hour as they attempted a variety of manipulations aimed at getting me to capitulate. If I weren't so frustrated, I would have agreed that I had a better chance of catching Melchor with them than without.

We pulled out of the garage sometime after 9 p.m. with a gray, starless sky overhead. My stomach roiled at the thought of arriving at the house. Of the six years that I'd been with Beth and Peter, we'd rented together for the past four.

Olivia exited the gate and turned onto a quiet East

Deer Valley Drive. "You are as intransigent as your profile suggests."

My eyebrows lifted, but I refused to discuss the recruitment offer or the Red Aegis. "What else does my profile suggest?"

"That you are impatient. You once drove to Palm Springs to get a file that hadn't been scanned into the system by an FBI agent there."

"Weather was good for a bike ride."

"It was an eight-hour round trip."

"The agent had promised the file for three days." I adjusted my position in her tin can of a car, feeling like I sat at my niece's tea party in a chair the size of one butt cheek.

"You are intolerant of neglectful behavior, among other traits you consider negative, but especially any work product you judge as 'lax.'"

Perhaps I overused that term in my reports, but shoddy, mediocre, or rubbish sounded less professional. I grunted.

"You are self-confident, often with good cause, as your perception and results excel. It is no wonder that Mika wants you on the team."

I grimaced, biting my words. We were getting close to the dense development where I lived. "How about you? What's your profile? Analytical but emotionally unavailable?" My lips twitched.

Olivia remained silent, her face expressionless.

We turned at my intersection. Streetlights lit the sand-colored houses as we navigated through them. Only now did I notice that she hadn't used any navigation on her phone.

Despite the dread and reluctance to step into our house, I made an effort to exit Olivia's little car quickly. The attempt proved clumsy.

"It was a pleasure to meet you, Zachary Graves. I look forward to seeing you again." Olivia's words had me frowning as I twisted my body out of the seat.

I'd already been ruder than necessary, so I just shut the door with a gentle push, then turned to face Beth's blue Prius parked in front of our garage. The security light had lit with the motion of Olivia's car.

She drove away, and I remained in the street. Three houses down, two neighbors talked and laughed, their banter stirring envy inside me.

Our house was dark, closed for our vacation. Of new, single-story construction, it tucked into the tightly packed community like it belonged, but now it appeared alien to me. Memories hung from every dry bush and on top of the stones we'd placed along the drive. *Can't stand out here all night.* I shuffled and took resolute steps onto the sidewalk before crunching through the gravel. I reached the sun-bleached walkway to our front door, passing the cactus that Peter always cut back. Everything would remind me of them.

The cooler air inside smelled of Beth's oil paints. My throat thickened, and I let my face crumple. Tears came too easily. With dead steps, I trudged through the living room toward our bedroom and stripped off my clothes. Everywhere my eyes set brought painful reminders: Beth's suit, dry-cleaned in plastic hanging from the door; Peter's latest script lying on the floor beside the bed; and the over-filled hamper. I stumbled into the shower, unable to stop crying.

I let hot needles of water dig into my back for longer than necessary to simply remove the sweat. When I emerged, I moved with urgent purpose. I pulled my running shoes from the edge of the closet, and I sat with measured intention on the bed to don socks. *I'm moving.*

Guilt surged, but I couldn't live with their memories, nor ghosts.

Tonight I needed to run. I'd take a couple of hours on the street and hope it would be enough to let me sleep. Tomorrow I could move forward.

Running shorts on, I strode past the reminders in the living room to the kitchen and filled my water bottle. From there, I retrieved my earbuds and set my phone to a Beck playlist.

I didn't even lock the door when I ran out of the house.

CHAPTER

FIVE

My phone buzzed on the bed beside me, waking me from the nightmare. I sat up on sheets still damp with my sweat from the run last night. Swollen from crying, my eyes took a moment to focus as I lifted my cell. *Mom.* How would she react? Hard and practical, or supportive?

"Zach. I'm so sorry. Anne called me. Why didn't you contact us?" Her voice wavered outside of her reserved tone, surprising me.

Anne, Beth's mom, must have been notified sometime in the afternoon, along with Peter's family. I rubbed my face, resting an elbow on my leg and staring at the rug. "The DRC had me most of the night." I answered the question before she could pose it. "A ghoul."

My mom sniffed in surprise, then asked with a cautious, tentative pitch. "How?"

"A ward." I rose, rolling my shoulders. "An arcane ward."

"Oh." A dreadful pause hung between us. "Are you in danger? We can get you to grandfather's property in

Minnesota." Her tone returned to its no-nonsense, steely tone.

"No," I said too abruptly, then tried to smooth it over. "The DRC is investigating."

"People die while the DRC investigates. They just lost one of their own." Her voice shifted, commanding. "I'll call in and we'll drive up north."

"No, Mom. I'm heading in to work." I winced. "I need to keep my mind off everything. Besides, there's no place safer."

"Zachary, be sensible." She paused. "What are you planning?"

"Nothing," I lied. "I just can't be here. I'm going to have to move." I stared at the window and the hint of a streetlight that seeped around the shade. "Let me get ready for work."

The silence dragged on long enough that I checked my phone and battery. It was low, but connected.

"Call me. Don't go through this alone."

"I'll call."

When I hung up, I jacked my cell into a battery pack to charge. Luckily, I'd put my earbuds on the charger when I'd finished my run around midnight. I played Nine Inch Nails and stepped out through the back sliding doors into the early morning darkness. The motion light clicked on. Lost in the music, I started my morning workout.

Two hours later, I rode my yellow 2002 BMW R1150GS, dubbed Bumblebee by Peter, past the FBI building, turning at the intersection. The Consociation clustered its departments in one area, likely for security reasons. I wasn't privy to those decisions. They housed the SDS behind the front of a tech company with plenty of parking.

I stopped my bike by the entrance, feeling the morning heat soak in as I stepped off. Helmet in hand, I studied the cars already parked. Izzie had arrived early, as usual, but I didn't see Angel's pickup. I'd have to move quickly. Most would not have heard about the attack yet, but upper management would know from Mika's inquiry. I had a limited amount of time before human resources got a hold of me and closed me out.

As I moved inside the doors, Anne called. My chest tightened as I ignored it. We'd have to talk at some point, all of us, just not today.

My footsteps echoed in the two-story lobby, and the security guard at the desk nodded and smiled. We knew each other by sight, but not by name. I strode with confident, unhurried steps for the elevators, digging out my key card.

Pasty pale despite the Arizona summer, blonde Izzie sipped at a mug as I turned the corner of our row of cubicles. She'd already removed her suit jacket, leaving herself dressed in a button-down white shirt and dark slacks. Her eyes widened. "What are you doing here?"

My heart skipped, but I kept walking to my desk.

"God, Zach. I just heard. What are you doing here?" She repeated the question as she took quick steps with a steaming, near-full coffee.

"I couldn't sit in the house." I re-used my lie from earlier in the morning, hoping it would get me the few minutes I needed.

Izzie hugged me, an oddity in itself. It proved awkward with a coffee in her hand and a helmet in mine. "God, Zach. I don't know what to say. You've got to be devastated."

One part of me was. "I'm going to dig in," I said, needing to move before they kicked me out. "It hits me in waves." That much was true.

She pulled back, nodding a bit too fast. "Yeah, I imagine."

After five years working in the same row, we were close, but drinks-after-work close. Angel and Izzie liked to dance, despite our varied choices in music. She didn't know me well enough to guess what I might be up to. After two more rounds of awkward statements, she let me dive into my cubicle.

As my station booted up, I stood and peered about the room, peeling off my thin backpack. The cubicles would fill by nine. I lifted my work phone off the cradle, placed it on the desk, and tapped four to speed dial the Consociation archives. It would cycle through their menu without end.

When my monitor blinked into life, I sat and navigated straight to my messages, digging out the one from my FBI liaison in cybersecurity. My target had attempted to hide his involvement through a company he'd created. On my pad, I scratched, "Michael Cherney." I jotted down the date the website opened, then Cherney's address, email, and phone number.

Two cubicles down from mine, Izzie's phone rang.

I deleted the email, then the entire contact. They could all be retrieved, but it might delay them a step at least.

"Zach. HR wants you."

"Got it," I called back.

I closed the screen, then pulled up a file on a dead lead to a different case from two weeks prior. In my heart, I knew the DRC wouldn't be fooled, at least not for long.

After one last glance, I ripped off the paper with Cherney's information and stuffed it into the back pocket of my slacks. *Reno*.

I had an arm through my backpack strap when I heard Izzie's muffled voice speaking to someone.

Angel swore.

With my helmet in hand, I exited the cubicle, turning to let Angel smother me in a hug with his wide shoulders. He shoved his face against my neck, mustache tickling as he spoke. "Oh, man." I could hear the tears in his voice, and nearly succumbed myself. "I'm so sorry, man." His suit jacket smelled of aftershave.

"Don't. You'll get me going, and I need to head up to HR." I closed my eyes, hating to play my friends. If I didn't end up dead, we'd talk it out over a drink.

He pulled back, wiping tears off his light-brown cheeks. "I'm so sorry," he said again. What was there to say? "You need to go home, take care of everything."

"Yeah, maybe." I pointed to the floor above. "I'll check in soon."

My two friends watched as I beat it for the elevators. *Cherney. Reno.*

Dad flies a lot for his work, so I had a contact for a travel agent in my phone. Before I climbed on my bike, I had a flight to Reno booked and an Uber on its way. Helmet unstrapped, I rode to the business that fronted my mom's Consociation department and parked in the back where it would take days for the DRC to find it.

Leaning in the shade while I waited for my ride, I planned my activities in Reno. The Red Aegis used a triad structure; that much we knew. Michael Cherney would have three connections: two that he worked with regularly, and a link to another triad.

My ride came quicker than I expected, but I jumped in, eager to get started, even if my flight didn't leave for four hours.

"A stop first at Quick Pik Towing," I said, handing the woman a twenty.

She took it. "Still going to the airport?"

"Yes." I forced an excited smile.

With a shrug, she returned the smile and kept the twenty. After a minute to look up the address, it took two more to head back to the intersection and down the road.

My focus glazed out the window. I hoped human resources would assume I'd gone home. What I didn't know was how connected they were to the DRC. *Just one step ahead.* If I could get to Cherney before them, I had a chance to unveil the entire triad.

When we pulled up in front of the towing company, my suitcase waited by the front door. I couldn't bring a weapon in my backpack, so I had to have a checked bag. The ride there had been a bitch, with the case strapped to the back, but I didn't want anyone at work to see it.

Ramon waved to me through the window as I grabbed it.

Half an hour later, I unlocked my gun case for the attendant and had clearance to repack it in my bag. From there, I had almost three hours to find out everything I could about Cherney while waiting for my plane to board.

I turned off my cell. Laptop warm on my lap, I used a new Google account to search for Michael Cherney, with little success. A pleasant woman in her late thirties tried to engage me in conversation from two seats down.

"Reno?" she asked, tucking back a strand of brown hair.

"Yes, yourself?" I opened tabs from my search, hoping to find some mention of the city to narrow it down. In another, I dropped in the address, hoping something might come of that.

"For a couple days, to meet up with the girls. Then the weekend at Lake Tahoe. A lot of kayaking."

"That sounds like fun." It did. I held back a frown,

remembering times with Beth and Peter, especially a midnight in Zephyr Cove where we'd rented a cabin.

Cherney proved difficult to find as a couple of famous people with the name took up a lot of the search. The address yielded a slew of real estate links, one with some interior views.

"How about you? Business, pleasure, gambling?" she asked.

"Business." I liked that the woman separated gambling from business or pleasure. Beth had avoided the activity after some poor decisions during her freshman year at ASU.

"What do you do?"

"I'm an analyst." Truthful, without disclosing too much. "Yourself?"

Fifteen tabs open, and I had one possible lead on a young man with dark hair who obviously forced his smile for a LinkedIn photo in the Reno area. I went with it and jumped to the insurance company he worked for.

"I process funding for a Toyota dealership." Her voice held a hint of embarrassment. "I'm still working on my accounting degree — when I can."

If I had the right Cherney, he'd be forty-two, and I guessed his picture to be from when he was thirty. I kept digging, hoping to find a recent photo.

Engaged in my search, it took a while before I realized the conversation had died off. I spent the better part of two hours researching. Conflicted, I wished I could have taken five more minutes at my desk, but knew the DRC would comb through my activities. With a couple of hours ahead of me on the plane, I filled my water bottle right before boarding.

I tried to nap on the flight, but nightmares encroached on my light level of sleep, snapping me awake. Stuck in a tiny seat with little to do and my own thoughts, I ached to reach Reno, though I planned to take it slow when I got there. With his work and home address memorized, spending the afternoon scoping out my target first seemed like the best plan. If I had the same resources as the DRC, I might have plotted a different course.

My eyes flicked open at the attendant's voice over the speaker. "Eighty-three degrees and sunny. Welcome to the 'Biggest Little City in the World.'"

Behind a young couple and an excited five-year-old girl, I ambled down the ramp into the airport. The bustle of the terminal echoed ahead of us.

The agent at the exit appeared embarrassed as she waved the young family ahead. Two security officers focused on me. "Zachary Graves?" one of the men asked.

I hesitated. "Yes."

"We need to go over your baggage."

People murmured behind me, and I stepped forward, shifting to the side. "I declared the weapon and ammunition."

"Follow us."

My lips pursed, but I complied, trudging behind one of them and ignoring the curious stares from our sudden audience. I'd never carried a firearm on a flight, so I might have messed up some detail. However, their guidelines had been specific, and I'd purchased the correct case years ago. The delay wouldn't prove worrisome for my plans, but I disliked it when something went amiss.

Close to the gate, the guards diverted me through a locked door that led into a beige hall. They opened a door, gesturing for me to enter.

Mika smiled, elbows on a white table. "Hey, Zach."

CHAPTER

SIX

I faltered, and a guard stepped closer, as if I'd try to run back down the hall.

"This is harassment, Mika." Not that I had any recourse.

Dagen stood to the side, legs apart in a ready stance, red hair bright under the lights, and a raging scowl on her face. Olivia watched me from over Mika's shoulder.

Mika waved me in. "Just a reminder. Thank you, gentlemen."

As I stepped inside, one of the guards pulled the door closed behind me. A musty scent hung in the stale air. I clasped my hands and stood motionless and silent at the table.

With a false smile, Mika shifted back a strand of pink hair. "Michael Cherney, eh?"

My nostrils flared, but I gained control of my expression. "Yes." How had they dug that up and gotten to Reno before me? My chest hollowed.

"What exactly is your intention? I don't believe it is a vengeful killing."

"Is that what my profile says?" I couldn't keep the bitter edge out of my voice. Their presence crumbled my plans. My eyes flicked to Olivia, but she remained curious and sharp-eyed, without any other tells. "What's *your* intention?"

Mika leaned down with a languid motion and retrieved a file. "I'm not at liberty to say. Protocol. You understand."

They didn't have information about the Red Aegis yet. I nearly smiled. Instead, I stood silent and impassive.

"What is your intention?" Mika repeated, opening the folder, but keeping it tilted so I couldn't get a glimpse. They flicked a sheet, waiting for me to respond, but I didn't. "I think you intend to interrogate the suspect. A task better left to a dragon-shifter, don't you believe?"

I frowned, and Mika continued. "They opened Tarus. That allows the Consociation specific avenues of investigation. What was your plan? A light crushing spell to apply pressure?"

My knee wavered, betraying me. *I want him to hurt.* My lips twitched at the idea. I rarely considered violence as an option, but my emotions swirled like a tornado when I thought of the man. I'd focused on capturing the entire triad, just to diffuse my momentary lapses of lust for revenge. If I could wrap up three of the Red Aegis, maybe four, then I might be sated. *Might.*

"Can I go?"

Mika leafed through another sheet. "We could do better together."

Dagen shifted and glared at Mika.

"Done?" I asked.

With a sigh, Mika closed the folder, snapped the edge against the table, then set it down. "Fine. Don't get in our way, Zach. They're holding your baggage at claims."

I moved to leave.

"Oh, turn your phone on. You've got a bunch of messages. Mom and some friends. One is from your supervisor at the SDS. You've been suspended. Indefinitely."

Not surprising. With a deep breath, I opened the door.

"He's clear," Mika called to the guards in the hall.

I stormed through the airport, was too brusque with the attendant who held my luggage, and didn't slow until I sat in my warm rental, a tiny Dodge, waiting for the air conditioning to make a difference. *I won't kill him*, I told myself. My threat might be to fold him into Tarus, bound, but I wouldn't do it. Cherney might deserve it, but I wanted everyone he knew from the Red Aegis. Would the DRC go that far, or just stop with him?

My head dropped until my chin rested on my chest. I turned on my phone.

Mom had called twice. William, my bandmate, texted his condolences, looking to meet up. Izzie didn't leave a message, but I had one from our department lead that I hadn't listened to. Anne had left a message.

"Honey, I know you're a mess right now. The police have only said it was an animal attack. When you're ready to talk, we need to understand. I'm working with Peter's father on the funeral. Call me when you can."

I brushed the tears away, trying to swallow. What would the DRC put out for a story? A mountain lion? *Black bear.*

I cued up Nirvana and linked my cell to the car, blasting my thoughts away. Halfway to the address of Michael Cherney's office, the air conditioning caught up. When I reached the parking lot, the churning in my stomach from the DRC ambush had faded.

The visor had a small mirror, so I leaned the chair back and pulled an illusion spell from Mer. Years of childhood pranks on siblings had honed my skill, so I replaced my dark stubble with shaved cheeks and a mustache, widened my nose, and set my irises to a pale blue. For the black curls of my hair, I spread a looser wave of dirty blond. My own mother wouldn't recognize me, unless I spoke.

From my luggage, I pulled out the polo shirt, clipboard, and manila envelope on which I had jotted "Michael Cherney," and swapped my T-shirt for the polo. I shut off Nirvana in the middle of their song, "Lithium," and hopped out with my props into the heat.

As I entered, the woman at the front desk put down her cell and smiled. "Good afternoon."

"Hey," I fanned my face with the clipboard. "I'm looking for Michael Cherney."

She tilted her head and pouted apologetically. "Sorry, he's out today." Her eyebrows rose as she lifted a hand. "Want to leave something for him?"

I returned her pout. "Can't. Need his signature. Do you know where he is, or when he'll be in?"

She sighed, poking at her phone. "Maybe check back tomorrow?"

With a smile, I studied her. This wasn't gatekeeping; he wasn't in. "Fair. I'll be back."

My face dropped as I turned and marched out the door. *House.*

I had better luck at Cherney's residence as I pulled the same pretext. He wasn't home, but his neighbor, an affable woman in her forties, happened to pull up as I walked up the steps. I tugged at Dur-Alf and Mer to see if he'd set wards, which he had, then knocked while she unloaded groceries. With a flick, I dropped Haven, lighting her up in ghostly white in the drive and her cat in her window, but nobody in Cherney's house.

"He's been gone over the weekend." She pointed to the empty driveway.

"Mr. Cherney?" I turned with an earnest smile.

"Yes. I don't know when he'll be back." Arms full, she closed the hatch of her SUV. "Not that we talk. I just happened to look outside when he piled a suitcase in his car."

Perfect. All I needed to determine for the moment was that I had the right address. "I'll try back. Thank you." I strode back to my rental and tossed the clipboard onto the passenger floor. Phone in hand, I feigned making a call while I studied the front of his house and his neighbors. A wince crept over my face as I calculated the hours since the attack. He'd had plenty of time to return home. Did he know he had failed to kill me?

I loaded the address of the hotel that the travel agent had booked and switched to Smash Mouth for the drive. A creeping fear crawled up my spine. *What if Cherney is waiting in Phoenix to finish the job?* Since I'd come to Reno, I'd move forward.

As I drove, I admonished myself for not checking for wards when I'd gone home after the attack. It would have been the perfect time to catch me unawares. I'd have to be careful. Between thoughts of Cherney and the DRC, my shoulders tightened. *Do they know where he is?*

When I got my key card for my room, I tugged at the realms before I entered, feeling every bit as paranoid as I acted. My plans earlier today felt withered and pale since Mika had accosted me. I dropped onto the bed and stared at the ceiling, fighting a wave of futility.

I forced myself to respond to my work, via email, and texted back William, trying to keep the slivers of my life intact. Part of me wanted to burn it all, but that would never get rid of the hole Cherney had left in my soul.

Two hours later, after a day of little more than snacks, I searched for a sushi place nearby, grabbed my keys, swapped my shirt, and headed down to my car. My phone rang as I stepped out of the hotel, but I ignored it, not recognizing the number.

It stopped after three rings, then dinged with a text.

THIS IS MIKA. ANSWER.

As I read the message, Mika called me. They had no reason to keep bothering me.

Whoever gets to Cherney first. I stomped toward my car. "What?"

"Do you know a James Hilderbrand?" Mika asked.

My steps slowed. "No. Why?"

"Tim Blanchard?"

"No. Should I?"

"Maybe."

My face tightened into a frown. Yet again, Mika wanted to show me that DRC had better resources than I did. We both knew it. "Leave me alone, Mika." I reached for my car, then paused. With a pinch, I tugged at Dur-Alf, and on my door, the blasting ward glowed moss green.

Stunned, I froze, knowing two things. Cherney was in Reno. He knew I was as well. My hand lowered, and with my thumb, I hung up on Mika.

CHAPTER
SEVEN

After I disarmed the ward, I checked the car three times before I stood twelve feet away and opened the door with a lifting spell of the water blue realm of Mer. I couldn't walk everywhere in Reno, but I'd been shaken by the simplistic efficiency of the arcane sigils. The Red Aegis had impressive knowledge.

I frowned at the rental while I baked in the afternoon heat. The odor of baked asphalt dominated the other smells of the city.

The car didn't explode when I started it up, nor on the way to get sushi, so I replayed Mika's call in my head. Were James Hilderbrand and Tim Blanchard in Cherney's triad? Had the DRC gotten that far ahead of me? Mika could be baiting me, or the names had come up in their investigation.

My grip on the steering wheel tightened in frustration as I considered playing along with the DRC. Olivia had been right; I could be stubborn. Was that my problem with them?

I didn't intend to kill Cherney, though I imagined

hurting him in the capture. In the end, I'd release him to the DRC, along with the rest of his triad if I could squeeze the information out of him.

I don't trust them.

That wasn't true. I wanted to be the one to hold his life in my hands.

As Soundgarden cued up on my playlist with "Fell on Black Days," I maxed out the volume.

Twenty minutes later, I ate sushi at a quiet bar and forced myself not to let my dark mood spill out onto the staff. Under dim lights and Japanese decor, the couples and larger parties laughing at tables burned a quiet agony into my soul.

William texted me.

Beer?

I put down my chopsticks, chewing on a piece of spicy tuna roll. He meant well. They all did.

Not tonight. Give me a day or two.

You okay?

As expected.

I paused, not wanting to talk with anyone from my life, but that wasn't fair to a friend.

I'll be moving. Keep an eye out for a place for me, I texted.

Between bites, we messaged back and forth, having gotten him on the topic of apartments. As much as I resisted, the distant discourse with a friend helped lighten my mood.

I still checked my Dodge for wards when I left.

That evening, I dug up a slew of Hilderbrands and Blanchards with variances in spelling, but lacked any real tools to link them to Cherney. The best I came up with had connections to Reno, so I jotted notes on them.

Around eleven I changed into sweats, a black T-shirt, a

side holster for my Glock, and a windbreaker to hide it. Feeling overdressed, I exited the lobby, surprised to find the temp had dropped to the seventies. I spent a frustrating minute checking my car for wards.

The pale green house three doors down from Cherney's had a for sale sign and space in the road out front for me to park. A blue haze of a television against the windows of the residence across the street offered the only hint of activity on this end of the block. Carried by the wind, the smell of someone's wood fire reminded me of camping.

I stepped around the Dodge and pulled at the watery blue of Mer. My skills fell short of using illusion for invisibility, but I could draw a fair shadow across myself. The absence of the moon and streetlights made the option a passable choice.

Cloaked, I walked down the asphalt, scanning the dark areas between the few yellow door lights. A dog barked deep in the neighborhood, punctuating the low murmur of residential Reno at midnight.

No car parked at Cherney's house, and with added frustration, I padded across the drive behind the neighbor's SUV. Where are you? So much for catching him at home.

Information. It made sense that he'd hide, knowing that I'd come for him. Arcanists tended toward libraries and even journals, so I'd make the best of my time here.

His dry lawn crunched under my feet. No lights lit the blinds in the window. Juniper hedges spiced the air. As I approached the steps, I tugged at Dur-Alf, highlighting a ward he'd placed over his door and casing.

"It was difficult to lose Phistrel," Mika said from a pace in front of me.

My heart lodged in my throat.

I stared directly at the point where Mika's voice had come from, but saw nothing.

"He was with us for only two years, but we were tight in that short time. Quiet, thoughtful, and always ready to help. A gentle human male, in my opinion." Mika spoke, hidden in a perfect illusion of invisibility. The air did not waver.

A masterpiece. "I'm sorry to hear." I stopped myself, prodding resentment to the surface. "What are you doing here?"

"I've got a dozen answers to that question. Let's go with 'waiting for you.'"

A part of me had considered that the DRC might try to catch me here, but I hoped my illusion and timing would alleviate my risk. I peered where the ward had shown. "Have you been inside?"

"Not yet. Waiting for you."

"Is this part of your recruitment?"

"The other is my own limitations. Merfolk can work with Dur-Alf; you know that. However, I'm clumsy when trying to unravel a ward. I'm less adept than other Merfolk."

"With Dur-Alf," I added, referring to her excellent illusion.

The steps scuffed with a light noise. Mika's voice emanated from higher up, as if they had stood. "Shall we go in? I can't pull Haven for piss, but I'm sure our target's not here."

I frowned, first because of the invitation, then trying to decipher her statement. "Do you know where Cherney is?"

"I probably wouldn't be here."

My emotions, curiosity, resentment, and frustration stumbled over themselves, so I just nodded sharply and tugged the ward apart. The simple alert would have told Cherney that we'd entered his house. An arcanist had to tie one such as this to a physical object.

When I pulled at Mer for an unlocking spell, Mika and I lit with a blue haze. With a Dur-Alf shield in place, I opened the door and took cautious steps, tugging at the realms.

The latch clicked shut. An acrid odor hung in the air, like fried electronics. When a flashlight lit the dark room, I jerked around. Pink hair glowed in the dim light; Mika had shed their illusion.

I dropped my own, arms resolving from the misty shadow. "Tim Blanchard. James Hilderbrand." Since it appeared we were working together on Cherney's house, I pried.

"Two men who died yesterday under questionable circumstances." Mika hadn't hesitated.

It didn't give me much. I cleared a blasting ward inside the front window. "Questionable?"

"Tim Blanchard died in a bar yesterday evening. A witness ran out of the establishment, distracting customers, who then found Blanchard stabbed in the heart with his own steak knife." Mika followed me at a safe distance, lighting up a bookshelf. "Statements described as being stiff."

I worked through the sparse room. The couch, table, and fireplace appeared clean and unused. "Witness. The one who ran out."

"Tracking him, along with others who left before the police arrived. They hadn't paid yet, so no credit cards for Neddie to follow."

Neddie had been the elder witch at the DRC office. We continued, passing the stairs leading below. "James Hilder-brand?" I asked.

Mika raised a finger, digging into a pocket and pulling out a cell. "Yes, Dagen."

I cleared the dining room, removing the wards on the windows. The hint of burned electronics had faded. Maybe I'd become accustomed to it.

"Bring them in. I'll come out when we're done. Hey, find us someplace open where we can sit and talk after."

Moving out of the ambient edge of the flashlight, I scanned the kitchen, peeling apart well-placed traps.

"I'm sure you're not." Mika's light moved toward my position. "James Hilderbrand died of a crushed throat. Found inside the door of his hotel room this morning. Time of death somewhere near midnight."

"Hotel room? He's not from Reno?"

"Phoenix." Mika waited for me to turn. "The names mean nothing?"

I shook my head, gesturing for us to continue. "Any sign of wards?"

"Yasmine doesn't have the body yet. The FBI is working to pull the two bodies from local enforcement."

Hilderbrand and Blanchard had to be Cherney's triad. "Any ties to Cherney?"

"We came to the information late this afternoon and plan to put his face in front of staff and customers tomorrow." Mika smiled. "Tracking you and searching for Cherney, or his body, has kept us busy."

My face flushed with residual frustration. "I won't kill him."

"The Red Aegis might, now that we're on his trail."

I sagged and winced. "The SDS released my files already."

"I set Pyre on them."

We moved on. "The lead out of the Atlanta DRC? How did that help?"

Mika chuckled without answering. Instead, they pulled out their phone and showed me a man with jet black hair like mine, but not curly, and a mustache. "Cherney." Three more pictures followed. One looked familiar, but I couldn't place it.

Once we cleared the upper level, we descended the stairs, where the reek grew sharper. I opened the door with a shield between us and a lifting spell. The frame exploded, though I'd gotten no indication of a Dur-Alf ward.

I swore, bumping into Mika as I pulled back.

Smoke curled out from the ruined opening. Splinters of wood dropped as I released my shield.

We were still on the stairs when Dagen jerked open the front door. "Mika!"

"We're fine. Simple booby trap."

Dagen turned on the room's light. "Heard that out front." Her face dropped into a scowl when she caught me looking at her.

Olivia glided in behind Dagen, peering at us.

With an extra tug at the realms, I raised another shield and led the way downstairs. I passed through the remains of the door frame. The explosive had burst from within. Wood crunched underfoot, and the smoke from the explosives hung in a haze about chest-height. The light switch didn't work. Mika shone the flashlight into the room.

Cherney blended the rune-covered style of a dark arcanist with a conspiracy techno-fanatic, though the monitors and computers at his desk were crushed rubble. Some pieces had ignited, and a fire extinguisher and dried foam told the rest of the story.

"That didn't happen just now," I said. "I smelled that from upstairs."

"Might still pull something from it. We'll package it all and send to Neddie."

I checked the room, surprised to find only three wards. Mika followed me, studying the books more than anything else. When I turned around from the sabotaged equipment, Olivia held a flashlight and watched me with intense eyes, and Dagen with a glare.

I'd come tonight to find out more about Cherney and possibly learn of his triad, if Hilderbrand and Blanchard could be connected to him. I knelt to inspect the surfaces of the destroyed computers, wishing I'd brought a flashlight.

A beam grew closer, and I turned to find Olivia approaching. "What are you looking for?"

"Their method of creating the ward." Arcanists used sigils, specialized markings that aligned with a realm.

"Ink, paint, wax, water, blood, something like that?" Olivia turned her focus to the crumpled surfaces.

"Most in the house appeared to be an oil mixture."

"Like the knights," she murmured.

"Who?" I asked.

Olivia shook off the question. "I've heard the markings do not even need to have a medium, that precise movements can construct the sigils."

I frowned. "Where did you hear that?"

She gave no expression of reticence, or anything beyond a stolid interest in her search, but she did not answer my question. "Creating a crushing ward to activate on touch is usually designed as a trap. What would an arcane do to implement such a violent magic?"

"It would be dangerous," I agreed. With a step back, I rose. "Can you point the light on the floor?"

I immediately saw the curved edge of a shattered clay coin. "There."

She picked it up. "A zum or srape. They inscribed it, then threw it to break on the equipment."

"A curse tablet." My lip twitched up, impressed with her knowledge of the archaic terms. "Most common among arcane followers of Iliodor."

"He does teach of their use."

My lips pursed, but I spoke. "The Red Aegis are believed to have splintered from his followers."

Olivia nodded, studying the clay shard.

Mika scraped one of the books back onto a shelf. "Where are we headed, Dagen?"

"A taco shop." Dagen's dour face tinted her voice.

"At midnight? Delightful." Mika turned to me. "Join us?"

I gestured to the room. "Shouldn't we finish searching here?"

"Why? What is your goal?"

"Find the names of his triad. Find Cherney." Why go to all this trouble and not get information?

"We'll more likely find that in a fish taco than in here." With a gesture, Mika stopped me from arguing. "He wouldn't write down Blanchard or Hilderbrand in a book, but have some code for them. I doubt he left an itinerary of his upcoming meetings. Any hint would be in that scrap pile you're standing next to, which Neddie will do her best to recover. Patience."

They were right.

Mika tugged out their phone, leading the way to the tattered doorway.

With reluctance, I followed the team upstairs to find a tall blonde woman equal to my own height. She wore a suit like Mika's and rolled a kit behind.

"Lord, Mika, you weren't kidding. A damned Adonis."

It took a moment, but when I realized she meant me, I flushed.

After a shooing motion, Mika buried the cell against

their suit and spoke a quiet rebuke. "Shush. Behave your-self. He's grieving."

The woman's smile disappeared, and she extended a hand. "Yasmine. Apologies. Condolences."

"I'm Zach. Pleasure to meet you."

"Hope so." A smirk edged onto the corner of her mouth. She released my hand and wrinkled her nose. "Did someone burn the smores?"

Dagen huffed, leading the way out of the door.

Outside, three black SUVs lined the street and driveway where a trio of FBI waited with emblazoned jackets. A fourth scurried from the side of the house. Younger than the others and closer to my age, he wore a grin as he glanced between us. "Agent Mika?"

Mika, still murmuring on the phone, nodded and pointed for Olivia to intercede.

The clean-shaven boy bounced on his toes, and the whole effect emphasized his bushy eyebrows. "I'm Agent Todd. I'm to liaison."

The other FBI took too much care to not notice us. I gathered they'd intentionally sent a rookie.

"I'm Agent Nordstrom. Maintain a cordon about the house and a twenty-four-hour presence until we've cleared the property. Explosives on site."

"I heard the explosion." He appraised me with a flick-ered glance across my dark sweats and T-shirt compared to the DRC's professional attire.

Olivia handed him a card. "Message me your contact information."

He beamed, digging for his phone. "Will do."

"Technician Isberg is processing inside. Please do not disrupt her. She will let you know if she has any requests, which she may. Please coordinate any questions or report any issues through me." Olivia surprised me with her easy lean into authority, but only because I'd grown used to her more quizzical nature. I admired her as much as Mika and guessed Dagen also had assets I'd not seen yet.

I scanned the dark neighborhood, noting a robed couple who stood on their step. Dagen glowered, and I flashed an apologetic smile. If I'd lost a partner, I might not be so open to a replacement within such a short time. My mother had always warned me that the DRC was a dangerous post.

"Ready?" Mika asked.

"Sure," I answered.

"Follow us." The team strode toward the street while I marched for my rental.

The corner taco shop we parked next to had outdoor seating beside what might be a busy thoroughfare during other hours. Fluorescent lights flickered overhead, with the lit sign rising from the edge of our fenced-in eating area and towering above. As Mika procured food and drinks, an occasional car motored past to the traffic light while I sat uncomfortably silent with Dagen and Olivia.

Mika had given me a wealth of information, but, as intended, it only proved how ineffective I'd be on my own. Blanchard and Hilderbrand had some part to play with Cherney, and I assumed they were his triad, but I'd prefer evidence. The DRC could provide that.

Despite the aroma of fresh cooking, I had little interest in eating; no doubt Mika used the pretext as an opportunity to talk, so I waited at the table. A wide sidewalk separated the table from the nearby lane, and I watched a gray sedan travel away from us going uphill on the opposite side.

Mika placed a laden tray between the four of us, then sat beside me. "I'd welcome you to the team, but I don't believe your mind is made up on that."

Dagen started to comment, but stopped at a look from Mika.

"So, what do you say to a temporary transfer to the DRC while we investigate the Red Aegis and your partners' murders? I've made the preliminary overtures to your department; there won't be a problem. This way, we don't stumble over each other."

Mika slid a fish taco off the tray, waiting for me to reply.

Part of me resisted, but my brain considered it the best option, for the moment. I stared down the street, watching the sedan make a U-turn and squinting as its lights shone in my eyes. "Temporary," I agreed.

"This is bullshit." Dagen stood, pacing to the rail that surrounded the dining area.

Before it reached us or the intersection, the car turned into the nearby motel and disappeared.

The only one of us eating, Mika mumbled an enthusiastic, "Good."

I leaned on the table, steepling my fingers and staring down the road. "What's your next move?"

"*Our* next move," corrected Mika.

Backlit from streetlights in the motel's parking lot, three dark figures sprang around the corner onto the sidewalk. Two wielded handguns, and the third an automatic weapon.

EIGHT

I jumped up, drawing everyone's attention. My right hand already grasped my weapon in its holster when the trio fired their first shot; it clanged against the sign's pole three feet away.

Red-haired Dagen leaped over the railing into the street, landing in a crouch that turned into a sprint.

A second shot from the attackers burst through a beverage on Mika's tray.

The three gunmen stood behind the lodge sign about eighteen yards away. The one with the automatic weapon had positioned himself farther along the sidewalk and took aim at Dagen.

I put a bullet into the attacker's center mass.

As the body spasmed, the rifle rattled out a spray of bullets, ricocheting on asphalt, the pole of a nearby streetlight, and eventually rising to ding into the traffic lights at the intersection.

Behind me, Mika's gunfire sounded while a binding spell flicked past my ear.

Olivia rolled over the fence, landing in a crouch to run

low and close to the brick wall of the building. From the beginning, the three members of the DRC had acted without hesitation.

One of the remaining attackers dove back behind the corner of the motel, and the second dodged behind the support that held the lodge's sign. While I aimed to go through the pole, something clattered to the ground, and a Dur-Alf shield sprung up.

He dashed behind the shield to join his partner, leaving their dead or dying cohort on the sidewalk. I held my fire.

Dagen sprinted to follow, four strides ahead of Olivia.

Belatedly, I pulled a binding spell and jumped over the fence behind them. The man I'd shot wasn't moving. I faltered, not wanting to see him. His mask had shifted down, exposing a strong nose and bushy brown mustache. *Not Cherney.*

With a curse, Dagen rebounded off the stagnant shield that she couldn't see. A gunshot sounded dully from the parking lot, and through ringing ears, I could make out the squeal of tires. Mika passed me.

When Dagen's yelp cut off, I turned my focus to the corner and followed the team.

Olivia shifted back into sight from behind the building, aiming her Glock at what I believed to be a dead man.

Someone I killed.

Dagen hung trapped in a binding in the parking lot with two tire tracks, the scent of burned rubber, and the attackers' gray sedan gone. Mika worked at the threads of the spell with clumsy attempts. I holstered my weapon, dismissed my binding spell, and released the one holding Dagen. She'd transformed enough to change her face, and claws hung from her hands.

"Be careful." I pointed to another clay coin on the ground, waiting for a foot to fall on it.

Mika patted my shoulder, flashing Mer, then called to Olivia, who stood by the body. "Get your excited FBI buddy over here. Leave someone at the house. I'll call in Yasmine."

Dagen had returned to fully human and paced toward Olivia, wary of the invisible shield.

I knelt, inspecting the curse tablet the size of a half dollar. *A blasting ward.* My ears rang, and my pulse hadn't slowed. I felt distant somehow as I picked up the clay coin with care, unsure how to dispose of it.

Onlookers were peeking out of motel doors, and a manager peered through a window. Mika and Olivia spoke from the sidewalk, their voices muffled.

As I turned to the team by the road, I recognized the feeling hanging in my chest. My mother's brother had taken me and a cousin on our first hunt when I was fourteen, and I'd killed my first deer. The disconnected sensation felt the same.

I forced myself to look at the body. The man had intended to kill us, albeit for my unmasking Cherney, but my bullet hadn't been searching for vengeance. Dagen might have been killed, running at him like she had.

Mika pulled down the dead man's mask, exposing his pale face fully, and took a picture.

I stood in the motel parking lot, watching the DRC do their job. All of them kept their eyes darting to scan the area, especially Dagen. Olivia patted down the corpse, finding nothing in the pockets but pointing out the placement of the hole I'd put in his chest to Mika.

With a shake of my shoulders, I moved to the standing shield that the gunman had created with the coin and unraveled it. Cherney could have been one of the others who attacked us; they were all masked and all males based on their shapes and movement.

Resolved to work through my emotions, I focused on the dead man. The numbers weren't adding up. If Cherney had been one of the two attackers who had gotten away, he'd have only two left in his triad, and we had three dead bodies. Even if I accounted for the contact Cherney should have with another triad, that totaled four.

"First time?" Mika asked me.

I frowned. "What?"

"Killing. Humans react differently than Merfolk."

"Um, yeah, but I'm processing." I twitched, unsure of how true my comment was. "I was thinking we had too many bodies."

"Agreed. Blanchard and Hilderbrand might have been innocents or part of another cell. Your reports and others mention a connection between triads."

A siren whooped down the street, and lights flashed red and blue as a local squad car bore down on Dagen at the motel driveway. Mika turned, raising a badge as the rest of the team did.

As an officer exited behind his door, hand on holster, Dagen shouted with a tone more like a curse. "FBI. Call it in." She shook her badge at the man, as if they could see it from that distance.

Something creaked behind me, and I spun, frightening the manager back inside. The lock clicked, and he backed out of sight. The whole night swirled like a surreal dream around me.

A second officer remained inside the car, watching us as he talked. Mika strode up, engaging them.

In a minute, we had another squad pull up and a full audience from the hotel residents with their cell phones out. Mika approached me and tucked a pink strand of hair away. "We've got a preliminary ID. Matt Fahne. Forty-eight. Owns a car dealership in Sparks, Nevada."

I glanced at the body where Olivia hovered. "Any connection to Cherney?"

"Neddie is working on that with all the known suspects. So far, we have Hilderbrand and Cherney on different flights from Phoenix on Sunday. Phones off. No other credit card activity. No emails." Mika trailed off as two black FBI SUVs drove up to the scene. "C'mon."

The excitable Agent Todd popped out of one, while two agents remained in the other. "Is this Cherney?" he asked Olivia.

As we arrived, Agent Todd smiled, but Olivia pulled his attention back. "Block these lanes at the intersection. Get the local law enforcement to help. We'll need a quick cordon to keep out reporters." Her deadpan expression never changed, and she never gestured for him.

He spun about, glancing at the corner where our food waited at the taco shop, then in the other direction. "I've got this." His cheery voice grated on me.

Phone in hand, Mika studied the agents sitting in their SUV and dialed. Olivia stood at Fahne's side near the weapon, peering down the roadway.

"Yasmine?" Mika asked. "I'd like to get this body off the street before we get some ambitious local deciding to argue jurisdiction."

Dagen looped toward us, refusing to catch my eye. In my youth, I'd been caught in binding spells before. They presented a terrifying loss of control. I flicked a sympathetic smile at her, but she pointedly ignored me.

"Understood," Mika said. "I'll get Everek to drive down."

The familiar name had me focus, trying to remember the context. It came to me. He was with the DRC in Montana. I'd dismissed most of the team's reports, since they had not spoken with Howard about the Red Aegis.

Mika continued to stare at the men in the SUV, but spoke to us. "Okay. Let's assume we've got Cherney and Hilderbrand working together to attack Zach over digging around about the website. Maybe Cherney kills Hilderbrand to keep it all quiet. Why come after us? What threat do we offer?"

"The Consociation won't stop hunting Cherney if we are dead," Olivia offered in a hushed tone.

"The Red Aegis are reported to have splintered off from Iliodor for multiple reasons," I replied in an equally low voice. "One is their use of Tarus. The other is a conspiracy theory that the Consociation, dragon-shifters specifically, have inhibited the ability for all humans to touch the realms as witches do."

Mika cocked their head in a shrug. "That theory's been floating about for a few centuries before this crew started popping up. They reference my species as proof, since all Merfolk see the realms."

"The dwarves are as varied in their propensity as humans." Olivia turned to me. "What does that have to do with the recent attack?"

"They actively seek to destroy the Consociation and likely saw this as an opportunity to strike."

Mika's lips flattened. "Then they might come at us again."

"Cherney has little to lose. Now that we have his identity, he's probably willing to die just to take down a few of us with him. I don't know his personality type, but the actions of the Red Aegis are considered fanatical." I released a long breath, looking at Fahne's corpse. "The others might not be as disposed to attack after tonight."

"It was a good shot, considering the lighting, distance, and speed," Olivia stated.

Good shot. I said nothing.

"One of the attackers tonight had arcane interest." Mika focused on me. "That does not mean Fahne did. Do you have any reports of the Red Aegis hiring mercenaries or assassins?"

I shook my head, then cleared my throat. "None. But our reports are limited, have been, until we found Cherney. I hope the SDS has assigned this to an analyst."

"They have," Mika assured me. "It might be a few hours before Neddie has any leads for us. Three hundred and eighty-four."

My eyebrows furrowed, trying to decipher the reference. "What?"

"That's how many downloads came from Cherney's site. Neddie is working with a team of Consociation techs to track and purge. It's time-consuming, but critical." They pointed to the clay coin I held. "You keeping that?"

Not warded. Even with a case, it could break and activate. I plucked the threads of Dur-Alf from it, leaving the markings to study later.

As Yasmine pulled into the motel parking lot behind us, I didn't argue the point. We had Cherney on the loose, at least two gunmen looking to ambush us, and thousands of rituals in the hands of kids and wannabes who could unintentionally open Tarus. And I killed a man, I thought.

With Yasmine backing in, I moved beside Olivia, ready to help load the body. "It's always like this, isn't it? With the DRC?"

CHAPTER

NINE

As I followed the DRC to their hotel, I didn't bother trying to untangle the bodies that had been found, or the body I'd left, into some manageable sense. I wanted Cherney and his triad.

Beck played over the car speakers, and I tapped out the rhythm on the steering wheel. Invasive thoughts pushed at me about the funerals and family members, but I swept them away. Cherney could hide from us in a hotel, if he had the cash, or at an accomplice's. We needed to drill down into his prior activity. *Before I poked the beehive. A move that cost me my family.*

Ahead of me, Olivia crossed a bridge, then paused in the middle of it. I checked the rearview mirror, then leaned to scan the street in front of us. At this late hour, not one car drove on the surrounding roads. An arch sported the city's slogan, "The Biggest Little City in the World."

Sightseeing? I thought.

We moved on, turned a corner, and pulled into the gated parking lot of a hotel.

My phone paused the music as Olivia called me. "Drive in behind me before the gate goes down."

I frowned, feeling like I was back in college, and complied.

With as little sleep as I'd had, my energy waned. I stifled a yawn as I grabbed my empty water bottle and locked up my car. Dagen and Olivia exited, the lock beeping from a click of the fob. Under the security lights, the SUV was empty.

"Mika?" I asked.

Dagen snorted. "She'll join us."

As we walked to the hotel entrance, Olivia moved to match strides with me. "Mika explained that you might be uncomfortable about the shooting. I apologize if I made you uncomfortable. An unnecessary remark, as you likely already recognize your handgun prowess."

Thanks? "No worries." My lips almost formed a genuine smile for the first time since the attack at the tent. Olivia was an odd one. I'd never worked with a vampire, but met two, and they'd been arrogant and self-important, nothing like her.

"A proper witch would have bound him so we could get actual information." Dagen walked ahead of me without turning to take her shot.

I took two breaths before I responded. "That would have certainly been a better plan."

Olivia's eyebrows lowered, but not quite into a frown. "If the binding had hit, then it might have worked out. However, a miss could have left you dead, Dagen. You were his target."

"Then you don't miss."

As we reached the entrance, they paused under the overhead lights, and I frowned, glancing about.

Mika appeared from the shadows of the massive pillars

that supported an overhang three lanes wide. "All clear. No one following us."

With a quick scan, I realized how different their day-to-day work was compared to my little cubicle. As my mother had cautioned, they were always under threat.

We wound through the quiet lobby and up the elevator to a luxurious suite. I appraised the wide room with two thick couches, a glass dining table with four chairs, and rooms to each side. The bathroom door stood open, exposing a massive shower. A desk by the window already sported a laptop.

My backpack sat on the speckled gray counter of the kitchenette, and my suitcase rested on the floor below it.

With a passing gesture, Mika spoke. "We grabbed your stuff. Cherney might know where you were staying."

"He does. Warded my car yesterday afternoon." I moved to my bag, checking for my laptop. "What do we know about Cherney's activities before I checked on the website?"

As Mika and Olivia moved toward the couches, Dagen stepped to the fridge. "Cherney was one of them," she said.

Mika stopped and twisted to look at her, waiting for an explanation.

Dagen pulled out a Sprite. "At least, the strongest male scent at the house matched one of the shooters." She sighed, retrieved a glass bottle of kombucha, and placed it on the granite counter in front of me. "Water or beer, Mika?"

"Water. How sure are you?"

Dagen juggled a couple of waters and her Sprite. "Very distinct scent, but maybe that shooter lived at Cherney's instead of him. It's not like I got to sniff the bedrooms. I would have, if I'd known they were going to jump us. Turds."

We had one werewolf in my department at the SDS, but we'd never talked beyond a greeting. How advanced was their scent?

I followed Dagen to the couches, opening my kombucha. Olivia and Mika sat on one couch, and as they took their waters, I paused, wondering if I should sit on the other. *With Dagen.*

She scoffed when she noticed me standing there and then sat. "I don't bite."

With a sip of decent kombucha, I eased onto the beige cushions and welcomed the rest. It had been a long day.

Mika drank, then frowned. "Should have grabbed the tacos." They waved off the comment and asked me, "What did you want to know about Cherney's activities? Why?"

"Details might give us a hint of his present whereabouts. Such as, if he likes comfort, then we can rule out dive motels and focus on upscale hotels. If he's living at the edge of his means, then his cash reserves might be low." I spent a lot of time tracking people, groups, and incidents based on their behavior or variances to predetermined patterns, only to hand that information to a DRC team, but now I felt I lacked the resources.

"I'll have Neddie include you on our reports." Mika pulled out their phone and began typing. "Olivia, you probably read one end to the other."

"Michael Cherney has a high arcane rating, though his activity dropped off the radar five years ago. He has frugal habits based on his credit card usage, but he pulls cash out of each paycheck, and we don't know what that is spent on. The amount ranges up to 50 percent of his income. His cell, internet, and credit usage portray him as a reclusive introvert with only the required connections necessary for work and household purposes. However, this could also be his intent to remain as anonymous as possible under potential scrutiny. I would imagine that we'll find that the computers he destroyed were those he employed for his actual internet activity and obfuscated their use." She peered at me with sharp eyes, as if waiting for me to comment, then continued.

"I didn't see one indication that he communicated with a single friend or family member. That is odd behavior for a human male of his age. He must have alternate means of communicating with his triad, since they would have stood out."

I'd noticed that the card he'd used to pay for the web hosting had been through a company bank account. "The company he created?"

"Solely used for the web services. He had two others, unused."

Dagen hopped up from the couch, shaking a nearly empty can. "If he had a buttload of cash, then he can hide as long as he wants."

"Cars, car rental, car insurance, driver's license are where we'll eventually get him," I murmured, unwilling to lose Cherney and wait until some traffic stop caught him. "But it makes the present situation difficult."

"James Hilderbrand did have more familial and societal contacts," Olivia said. "He pursued a more affluent lifestyle with a social media presence. His shallow interest in the arcane, as a youth, discontinued after college. Neddie hasn't alerted us to any arcane connections within his circle of acquaintances, but it is wider than it appears deep. His wife lives within the same society, and her closest friends are not in our database as arcane. Nothing I saw gave any indication that he engages in the craft."

I waited until she finished before I spoke. "He might have a similar setup to Cherney, just not destroyed."

Mika leaned forward. "We can't abandon Cherney for it, and I don't want to send in the local FBI. They could set off a hidden ward that would harm them or the wife. We'll plan on digging there when we're done here."

Olivia waited, and when no one else spoke, she continued. "Tim Blanchard works a local casino. He shares an apartment with a blackjack dealer and has a social media presence. His interest in the arcane rose to the level of tarot, but only as a consumer, not a practitioner. A small core of people forms his friends, including the witness who ran out of the bar when Blanchard died. We still have not found the friend, but it is likely a Devin Gough, who is now missing. Neddie promised we'd have a profile of Devin by the morning."

I rubbed my eyes. "Do any of you sleep?"

"After the case," Mika said.

Dagen peered through the curtains, letting in a sliver of a view of Reno, where the darkness sparkled with lights like stars. "Should we get back to Cherney's house? Do we know if Yasmine got the computers on the way to Neddie?"

"She did," Mika confirmed.

My eyes glazed, and I rolled my head, staring at the ceiling and pastel abstract on the wall behind me. Any of the bodies, or even the witness, could be Cherney's triad. Matt Fahne had come to the fight without ID or personal items, and hadn't used any arcane magic, so he might just be a hired gun. We needed to capture someone, preferably Cherney.

"We believe they are hunting us," I said, "and we know they found the location of my hotel." My lips twitched, unsure of my plan.

"You wish to set yourself up as bait?" asked Olivia.

I pulled my head up to stare at her. "Yes, it was an idea."

"Sounds brilliant," said Dagen with a smirk. "We can scrape up what remains of you after we take down Cherney and his buddies."

Legs stretched to rest on the coffee table, Mika tapped their water bottle against their lips. "It's a possibility, but we might also be wasting time."

Olivia shook her head. "We are experiencing an information bottleneck at the moment. Neddie is processing connections, and we've added Matt Fahne to her load. The computers will take a couple of hours to transport with more time needed to disassemble and attempt any extraction. We might be a few hours before we have one piece of new information."

"You're right," Mika agreed. "Beyond dodging about to an endless supply of Reno hotels, we have nothing to act on."

Olivia's phone dinged, and she dug it from her jacket.

I'd never been bait before.

Dagen cursed. "We'll need to dig out the comms. Hate them."

"Agent Todd messaged me that local enforcement just found a body matching our description of the gunman at the scene of a disturbance." Olivia turned as she spoke, rising from the couch.

Mika, who'd assumed a casual pose, popped up as if on springs. "Get the location. Have him secure that scene and body if we don't get there first."

The last to rise, I chased them for the front door. Had Mika's shot hit, and the partner just dumped the body? I could only hope that it was Cherney that the police had found.

CHAPTER
TEN

"What's the cause of death?" I asked as the DRC team burst into the hall.

Olivia typed as she jogged. "I'll ask. I need the location first."

"What are you thinking?" Mika ran toward the elevator alcove.

Along the well-kept hall of the hotel, I cringed at the noise we made, running past guest rooms, and waited until I reached the others to answer. "It might be your bullet."

"Nope. I saw it miss by about a quarter inch." Mika appeared sure, and I wondered at their vision.

Dagen paced to the window while Olivia focused on her phone. I drew a deep breath.

The elevator behind us dinged, and we darted inside among the mirrors and wood paneling. As we descended, my pulse rose with the team's eager demeanor.

"Vehicular homicide. Dark-haired, white male. Confirmed dead upon arrival." Olivia stopped reading, looking to Olivia. "Agent Todd is arriving on scene and will secure it from the local police. He has requested additional agents, but advises that it might just be him at the moment."

Cherney? Did I want the body we would find to be him? The elevator door opened to the lobby, and I strode at the full length of my long legs to keep up with the team. Vengeance, relief, and guilt swirled in my chest like a muddy river.

Mika waited until we were at the front doors to ask, "Yasmine?"

"I've alerted her on the address."

Dagen chuckled. "She must've been thrilled. Bet you got an earful."

Olivia turned to peer at her teammate before responding. "She texted an appropriate response, understandably concerned with her present tasks. There is one body in her SUV presently." Like an owl, her head swiveled to Mika ahead of me. "Yasmine requests FBI resources for storage. Should I have her liaison through Isaac?"

Dagen huffed. "As if he'd be up at this hour."

"Tell her, yes," answered Mika.

Olivia returned to her phone, taking quick steps across the asphalt without hesitation.

Isaac? How many people worked at the DRC in Phoenix?

As we reached their SUV, Mika pointed me to the seat behind the driver. Olivia unlocked the doors, and I jumped in to sit in the rear with Dagen. I'd left my water bottle upstairs. In Arizona, I never went anywhere without plenty of water.

We crossed the same bridge, and Olivia drove at the speed limit; the rush to the car had me believing we'd be blazing through the cities with flashing lights. The few cars traveling these morning hours moved faster than we did.

How did a vehicular homicide come to Agent Todd's

notice? "Did the FBI explain what they meant by matching our description?" I asked Olivia.

"They did not, but we described two men in dark clothing, at least one in a black sweat suit, wearing gaiters."

I'd only seen their silhouettes. One or all of the team had better vision than me.

We turned at an intersection, and the flashing blue lights ahead marked our scene. Police cars partially blocked the drive, and an officer only let us through after Mika rolled down a window and flashed a badge.

To the left, Agent Todd stood with a cluster of officers near a body on the asphalt. The brighter lights of the parking lot barely lit the area, but I could make out arrows pointing to the overhang of a hotel's entrance and speed bumps. Olivia parked so the headlights of the SUV shone on the group and left the motor running as we exited.

The officers shaded their eyes at our arrival, and one broke off to stomp toward us, despite Agent Todd trying to explain. Sweaty and red-faced, the balding man pointed as he opened his mouth.

Mika preempted a tirade. "Agent Mika, Special Agent in Charge. Do you have any witnesses?"

"Listen—"

"No time for a pissing contest." Mika gestured to a man dressed in a blue hoodie by the wall of the hotel, who shifted under the close attention of a bored police officer. "Is that a witness?"

I hadn't noticed either of them.

"He's a local bum. This—"

Mika jabbed a finger at me and Dagen, then the witness. "Get his statement."

Dagen smiled, appearing to enjoy the officer's fluster as Mika and Olivia strode past him toward the body. As we headed for the side of the building, I peered at the corpse;

it lay face down with a gaiter pulled down to the man's chin. He had a goatee, not just a mustache.

Unless Cherney grows facial hair quickly, it's someone else. Another name. Usually I didn't mind a long list of connections, but I wasn't sitting in my cubicle after a decent rest.

What might have been a witness appeared to be a young man with light brown skin and a cap on his head. He eyed us warily.

The white officer appeared relieved when we arrived, stepping to leave without a word.

"Thank you," I said to him.

Dagen gave me an odd look, then turned to our witness. "I'm Agent Whalen. This is Graves." She pulled out her phone and typed. "Can we start with your name?"

Surprising. She often came off rough, a little less so with me since the firefight.

"Lazlo Ramirez." He spoke with a light Hispanic accent and wet his lips after he spoke.

"Great, Lazlo, what did you see?"

He shifted, tugging at his thin jacket. "I mean, I told the other one, not much. I was walking down 6th. I couldn't help but see the two men running and the car." Lazlo stopped, gesturing with two fingers in front of his lips. "A reddish truck. SUV. I didn't see the make or plate. Told him so."

"Told the police officer?"

He nodded, smiling. "Yeah, him."

Dagen waited, then prompted. "So you see the vehicle. Is it chasing the two men?"

"Yeah, chasing. Trying to run them down."

"Did you see the driver?" Dagen asked.

"White guy." He nodded toward me. "They all was. The ones running tried throwing something at them, I thought they might be chips. Good casino chips to get them to stop and pick them up."

Curse coins. I glanced behind at the parking lot. If they'd tried a binding, an arcane binding wouldn't stop a vehicle. *I doubt* I *could.* We'd need to clear the lot and make sure none had survived intact.

"The driver was white. Hair color? Facial hair?" Dagen asked.

He shrugged. "I was on the sidewalk."

"Okay, so they run down the one man?"

Lazlo hesitated, then nodded.

"Anything unusual happen?" I asked.

His eyes flicked to the officer who had left. "You won't believe me, but he just froze like. One foot in the air. Like a cartoon." Lazlo swallowed and glanced away. "I must've been mistaken."

I waited for Dagen to ask the question. "Were the people in the vehicle throwing anything, like chips, back at the people running?"

He frowned. "I don't think so. But I was on the sidewalk."

I turned to where Mika, Olivia, and Agent Todd stood talking with one officer while the rest moved toward their cars in the parking lot. From the body to the street could be twenty yards, but the lighting wasn't good.

"What happened after the car ran into that man?" Dagen asked.

"It drove off." Lazlo pointed under the overhang and down the side of the building.

"Where did the other man go?"

He pointed to the entrance of the hotel. "Inside."

Dagen spun and let out an ear-splitting whistle, gesturing to Mika, then to the hotel doors. "Wait here," she said to Lazlo and burst into a run for the entrance.

I kept up as Mika and Olivia raced to catch up to us. As the automatic doors eased open at a slow pace, Dagen squeezed through.

Just inside the second set of doors, two employees pulled back from where they'd been leaning against the glass, watching the activities outside.

"Where did he go?" asked Dagen, in her normal, gruff tone.

A pale young woman pointed. "The casino." As Dagen took off toward an opening, the employee called behind her. "You'll need a key card."

I followed Dagen, yelling to the woman, "Open it!" When I turned the corner, a bright, illuminated "Casino" sign hung over sliding doors that Dagen easily pried open with her dark nails. When I reached her, I caught the edge and held it for Mika and Olivia.

The noisy, clanging room had few people and a matching set of doors on the far side that led into a lit parking lot. Whoever the second person had been, they were likely long gone. Despite the likelihood of his still hiding here after all this time, I joined the team and hurried down the rows of slots. Not one of the curious customers had black hair and a mustache nor wore a gaiter.

Mika stalked back into the lobby, gesturing the rest of us out. "Is there a manager who can get me security footage?"

As we stepped outside, Dagen headed for Lazlo. "I've got this. Stay with Olivia and the body."

Agent Todd had been joined by another agent, a woman who watched us approach. The team's SUV shone bright lights against their backs, shadowing their expressions at this distance.

I focused on the body as we walked, but asked the

questions rattling in my head. "We've got people chasing and killing the people who ambushed us. Are these others trying to stop them? Other Red Aegis? Does this make any sense?"

Olivia answered, her voice low. "It could be as you've surmised. We don't truly know how the Red Aegis organize, beyond triad cells. There could be an overarching governing branch that is trying to stop a rogue element."

They don't much like authority. However, Olivia could be right. I didn't much like authority, yet here I was, working with the DRC.

My phone dinged, and I dug it out of my pocket. I half expected a text from Mom or William, but not at this time of the morning. An unknown caller with a Phoenix prefix texted.

Open me.

They'd included a link.

Not likely. I frowned. *Who had my number?*

Olivia rattled off the number with a question at the end without having glanced at my phone.

Put off by her ability to read a situation, I snapped a side glance at her and answered, "Yes."

"Neddie." Olivia turned her sharp attention to me. "We have a program, like Slack or email, to receive reports. Mika would have authorized you to have access." She leaned in and whispered. "Please check the body for wards."

My attention returned to the beaming Agent Todd and the stern woman beside him. She wore a police vest and hooked both her thumbs at the armpits in silence. The sight of the body flashed a memory of the man I'd shot earlier. I winced and repressed the thought. As requested, I tugged at the realms, with no result. I shook my head as we came to a stop.

"I've got two more agents on their way," Todd said.

Too cheerful, buddy. I watched as Olivia knelt to check pockets.

The officer sniffed, but she didn't offer a comment.

Olivia pulled out a phone, handed it to me, and continued searching.

"Locked," I said.

With the rest of the pockets empty, Olivia stood and took the cell. "Neddie will crack it."

Two feet from the man's head, I spotted a broken shard of a clay coin. Black tire treads marked the speed bump beyond that, so I backtracked the trajectory of the vehicle toward the painted arrows in the parking lot. I didn't see any point in standing beside a dead body and exchanging grins with Agent Todd as the temperature dropped, so I strolled away in search of curse coins.

Before Yasmine pulled into the parking lot, I found four active clay chips with binding wards and deactivated them. I pocketed them along with the shards of five more.

I stood a few yards from the DRC, Mika having joined them, and watched as they worked. *We're no closer to Cherney.* The team with all its resources might eventually find who killed my partners, or not. I'd hoped they'd expedite my search. After a long day, a hint of futility nagged at my weariness.

I'd continue to play along, load Neddie's program and reports, even become bait, but I didn't belong with the DRC.

From the group clustered around Yasmine, who inspected the broken body, Olivia noted me watching and broke off to speak with me. "The victim is Jay Werner from Folsom, California, where he owns three restaurants. He's a practicing arcanist at age thirty-eight."

Lovely, a new name for the list. Werner. "Any connection to any of the others?"

"Neddie doesn't have any information on that yet. Mika has her working with Isaac to get the security footage from the hotel." Olivia pointed to my phone. "We've got more background on Hilderbrand. Also, there was a disturbance at the home of Devin Gough; it appears someone tried to kill him around three hours ago."

I tried fitting everything into a timeline, but couldn't. Even a pencil and paper would have helped.

A few minutes to get my thoughts together, that's what I need. With a forced smile, I jabbed a thumb at the team's SUV. "I'm going to sit down and get Neddie's program loaded. Check some of this out."

She nodded and spun to walk back to the DRC team.

Inside the running car, I leaned back in my seat and closed my eyes. *An odd bunch. I miss Angel and Izzie.*

CHAPTER

ELEVEN

When Mika opened the passenger door, I woke with a start.

Dagen's grin widened as she opened her door. "You snore like a lawnmower."

"Maybe to your ears," Mika said. "Thirty minutes will have done you good."

Olivia slid in, pulling down her seatbelt.

I checked my phone at 4:42 a.m., so I'd been asleep for almost two hours. "Sorry."

Mika twisted in their seat, smiling at me. "Don't be. Me and Dagen have been taking turns napping yesterday while we trailed you."

With a scrub of her red hair, Dagen feigned a study of my curls. "Hair's a bit lopsided. I think you've got drool in your stubble."

"Leave him be. I'm hungry. Find us a place that's open, Dagen, would you?"

Breakfast? My stomach had settled, but I fought guilt at taking the time to eat and sleep. My T-shirt was developing a funky, gym-locker scent.

Olivia hadn't moved to put the idling car in gear. "We don't believe we can use you to draw out Cherney at the moment. The images from the security footage, mainly those in the casino, give us a 74 percent chance that it was Cherney running out into the parking lot. We found his vehicle."

I straightened, frustrated that I hadn't considered he'd parked here. Mika studied my face as questions swirled through my foggy brain.

"Sending you a link to a casino," Dagen said from beside me.

"What did you find in his car?" I asked Mika. *Wards.* I could have been of some help, instead of crashed in the back seat. "Did he set wards?"

"I found two, and Yasmine cleared them for me."

Yasmine's a witch. It made sense.

Mika continued, "We identified little that would give us any indication of his present whereabouts, which is the most crucial focus. The car belonged to Jay Werner. A gray 2015 Toyota Camry." With a flick of their cell, they showed a picture of it. "Is that what our gunmen were driving?"

Olivia drove the SUV in a wide circle, heading for the exit. The body, Agent Todd, and Yasmine were gone.

I'd barely gotten a look from the seat at the taco shop. "Yes."

"Clean inside except for Matt Fahne's locked phone in the glovebox; weapons and ammo under the front seats."

Dagen snorted. "Bet they wish they'd kept them, when someone's trying to run you down."

"Yasmine will send the phone to Neddie; she'll crack it, among everything else we've piled on her. Stolen plate on the back. Jay Werner booked the room for this hotel." Mika paused.

My jaw tightened. *Why not wake me?* "Anything?"

"Blast ward on the bathroom door. Yasmine cleared it. Otherwise, she took Werner's clothes, phone, and bag, but other than an assortment of beard oils, nothing of note. No laptop. You didn't miss any details."

Despite their attempt to assuage my guilt for sleeping through the investigation, I ground my teeth in frustration. I fought demanding why they hadn't woken me; it wasn't their job.

What would Cherney do now? *No car. No home. No hotel room.* "We need to check Cherney's office."

Mika smiled. "Agreed. They won't open for a few hours. Everek will be here by then to help Yasmine. We should have some new information from Neddie soon. She's on silent mode at the moment. We've got a decent couch in the lounge."

"Lounge?" I asked, not missing the hint that even Neddie napped.

"A gym bro like yourself, you'll love it." Dagen had slouched down in her seat.

With a toss of pink hair, Mika rolled their eyes. "We've got a weight bench and treadmill. Showers. Kitchenette and table. Enough to break during cases."

A recruitment brochure? "Nice."

Mika turned and focused on their cell. I did the same, idly loading Neddie's program like I'd planned before I'd fallen asleep. By the time I pulled up the detailed report on Cherney, we'd arrived at an entrance to a casino attached to the resort. I piled out with the others in the gray twilight.

Inside, the bells and chimes of the gaming floor surrounded us. I wasn't surprised at the number of people glued to machines at this hour; I'd been to Vegas plenty.

As we wound through the clamor, I still felt we could

be doing something to track down Cherney. My job at the SDS had included plenty of long days tracking important clues, but I could eat and drink at my desk, only taking a break when my eyes failed. On the trail of a live person, I wanted to keep moving. *Not that I can't handle this.*

A woman ahead and to our left squealed as her machine rang out a win with an electronic replication of coins jangling into a bowl. Dagen laughed and yelled, "You got it, girl!"

My mood soured at the gaiety, envious of someone's happiness, and the reaction drove me deeper into a guilty, jealous funk. *I don't belong with these people.*

When the hostess greeted us, I trailed the team, but mustered a pleasant, "Thank you." In her thirties, she wore her sandy blonde hair in braids and shook them as she pointed our menus into the empty dining area. "Anywhere you like."

Dagen marched into the lead, heading for a soft-cushioned, circular booth. Mika and Olivia left me walking with the woman.

"Late night? Hope the tables were good to you." The hostess tapped the menus against her palm.

I adopted an affable expression. "It has been a long night, but we just got here. Quiet shift?"

She rolled her eyes. "Dead. One table of drunks since 1 a.m." We slowed as Olivia and Mika slid into the booth. "I'm out of here in a couple hours."

Dagen pointed me toward the middle, wanting the outside seat for herself. "Easy tiger. We're on duty."

The hostess blushed, and I maintained a flat expression, sliding in beside Olivia, though my grip tightened on my phone.

The booth could have fit six comfortably.

"Something to drink? Your server will bring them out." The woman smiled at Dagen.

I held my phone in my lap, under the table, opened the report on Cherney, and scrolled to gauge the depth. Neddie was efficient, linking onerous details like phone records.

When the hostess circled around to take my drink order, I asked about tea.

"Iced sweet tea, or hot? We've got a good selection." She noted my reaction to her latter statement. "We just bring the box out for you to choose from."

"That would be perfect, thank you." I nodded pleasantly, and when she moved on to Olivia, I focused on the reports.

Cherney had booked his Saturday flight to Phoenix late on Friday night via his home internet. Except for unanswered solicitations, his phone had zero activity from Friday afternoon until he turned it off Sunday morning, when it remained off. I dug through his sparse connection with the world outside of his work and considered the computers he'd destroyed. *He's connecting somehow, maybe piggybacking off a neighbor.* I hadn't checked for any extra routers or Wi-Fi extenders but should have.

Neddie's summary of Cherney's work communications and activity gave no hint of anything we could use, so I didn't dig into the details. I could save that for later.

Dagen didn't bounce, but her demeanor oozed energy. "Why do we always have to find one local jerk on these cases?"

I scanned Cherney's purchase of his flight home, made at the airport on Sunday afternoon, after Beth and Peter had died. His last credit card purchase had been a burger while waiting for his boarding call.

"People don't like to give up control, especially in the

enforcement profession." Mika had their phone out, perhaps scrolling through reports.

The program proved easy to navigate, and I pulled up Hilderbrand's report, focusing on his ticket purchase. He'd taken a different flight, booked Sunday morning, and left close to the time we activated the ward. Why had he even left his home and Phoenix? Did he fear being implicated in the attack on me? I skimmed a couple of his social media accounts, but he made no mention of leaving, so it hadn't been planned.

The waiter who brought our beverages had a long nose that suited his face and solid cheekbones under dark brown eyes. "I'm Billy, and I'll be taking your orders." He placed my cup and pot of hot water close, positioning the box of teas farther out but within reach.

I ordered an egg-white omelet with fruit, selected a bag of green tea, and resumed my search of Hilderbrand's file, grateful for the distraction from my emotions. Except for Dagen, the others appeared content to focus on their phones, perhaps reviewing newer reports.

"Don't suppose Cherney would be foolish enough to head back to work, do you?" Dagen asked.

No one answered, and I left Hilderbrand's report reviewed superficially, with far more I could dig into later. Blanchard's file included the police reports of the death, which I opened. As Billy set our plates in front of us, I paused on a section where one of the patrons noted Blanchard returning from the bathroom. The witness commented that Blanchard had passed two men at an end booth who were arguing in hushed tones.

From the comments, the patron suggested that the men were the killers, since one of them was near Blanchard when Devon made his escape, knocking down his chair in the act. I skimmed through the other witness statements.

We were alone when I spoke. "I think Tim Blanchard and Devin Gough are not involved with the Red Aegis."

Mika paused with a forkful of pink salmon. "Why?"

"Blanchard had just returned from the bathroom and passed two men who did not wait for the police to arrive. 'Two white businessmen. Neat hair. One had a mustache.' When asked about hair color, 'both had dark hair.' Cherney has black hair; Hilderbrand, dark brown." I scrolled back up the report. "Witness states that 'They seemed annoyed that — Blanchard — walked by them during their conversation. When the other guy ran out, one of them was standing nearby, but I didn't see him stab — Blanchard.' I think Blanchard heard something he shouldn't have."

"Do you think he might have told Devon Gough what he heard?" Mika asked.

I shrugged. "Be a good reason to try to kill him later."

Olivia, who'd ordered a Danish and picked at it, spoke. "If you are right, and the logic seems thin, then they likely would not want to risk the chance."

"Agreed." Mika ate a forkful of sliced salmon, ignoring the bagel. "Anything else?"

"Yes. I think we need to look for a Wi-Fi extender at Cherney's house. He barely uses the internet, which is odd considering having multiple computers and monitors. I'd bet he's piggybacking off a neighbor. If so, we can track his activity."

"Olivia, have Agent Todd do a walk around the building and see if he sees any unusual equipment. Make sure he doesn't touch anything. I'll see if Yasmine collected any routers or such."

Halfway through a bland, unseasoned omelet, William messaged me.

Stopped by the house. Figured you'd be working out this time of the morning. Guess you're asleep. I'm outside.

Sorry. Out of town, clearing my head.

I frowned at the lie, but I couldn't tell him I was hunting Peter and Beth's killers. He'd be worried.

Fair. Let me know when you're back. Let me know about the funerals. I'll go with you.

Will do. Thanks.

I put my cell down with emotions swirling and stabbed at a piece of cantaloupe.

Mika had returned to their phone. "I think you're right, Zach. If the four had known each other, then trouble might have started earlier, not when Blanchard went to the bathroom. I'd like to get Cherney and Hilderbrand's photos in front of those witnesses, maybe later today."

With a conscious effort, I stifled any reaction, but felt pleased that I'd added something to the investigation. If we scratched Blanchard and Gough off our list of Red Aegis, it left Cherney's triad and one extra, who might be his contact to another triad. That made sense, and left Cherney alone.

Olivia's phone rang. "Agent Nordstrom," she said. Her eyes widened, and she motioned for us to exit. "We'll be right there."

I slid out behind Dagen.

"Agent Todd has been injured in an explosion outside Cherney's house," Olivia reported.

A chill crawled up my back. I'd only checked for wards inside. The others led the way, Mika flashing a badge to the hostess, promising future payment. For the second time in less than a week, my questions had led to people getting hurt. First, Peter and Beth, now my question about Cherney's potentially stolen Wi-Fi had gotten Agent Todd injured.

CHAPTER

TWELVE

We ran through the casino with lights flashing, bells ringing, and patrons barely noticing us with their drinks, coins, and smokes. I fought a heaviness that weighed on my shoulders and chest.

The gray twilight of morning lit the edge of the sky. The street outside the parking lot had already grown busier.

As we piled into the SUV, Mika asked, "Any details on Agent Todd's status?"

Olivia belted herself into the driver's side. "An ambulance has been called, so I assume he is alive. They stated injured, not killed."

As before, Olivia drove the speed limit, but this time I had the urge to break it and race to the scene. It didn't matter, as the ambulance had likely already taken Agent Todd, and I could do little more than a thorough search of the outside for wards. I might be able to satisfy my curiosity about whether Cherney used a neighbor's Wi-Fi.

Mika spoke on their phone. "This is Agent Mika out of Phoenix. Yes. Yes. I'm going to need some vests after the incident over on Virginia Street. Yes, perfect, we'll pick them up there. We're heading there now. Thank you."

Dagen cursed. "I hate vests. I feel like a sausage."

"Better than a sponge for bullets. I didn't like you charging without protection last night." Mika's tone held a firm but quiet rebuke.

Traffic built at the intersections as early workers rushed to their weekday jobs. I would have been working out. My mind recoiled, not wanting to remember Beth and Peter's morning routines.

"I think we can be fairly confident that Hilderbrand is either in Cherney's triad or his contact with another triad. What I don't understand is why he traveled to Reno?"

Mika texted, but tilted a bob of pink hair to the side, answering, "Perhaps their backup plan included leading you to Reno."

I stared out the window, letting the cars and buildings blur. Cherney found out I'd outed him and hoped to kill me at the campground before I got the details. If he had, one of the people in my department would have picked up the trail, so he still had to burn what he could. He'd sabotaged his equipment before he left. "Once I survived, Cherney knew I'd scope out his house. I'd bet someone followed me from there to my hotel."

Olivia spoke. "Hilderbrand scheduled his flight before the attack occurred. He might be one of Cherney's triad. Since you exposed Cherney, they could have intended to meet and plan how to deal with the SDS and DRC investigations."

Her suggestion made more sense than anything I'd come up with.

My phone dinged with a message from my dad.

TAKE THE TIME TO GRIEVE. CALL ME WHEN YOU CAN.

I'M HEADING BACK TO PHOENIX THIS MORNING SO I CAN BE THERE FOR THE FUNERALS AND YOU. I LOVE YOU.

LOVE YOU TOO, DAD. THANKS.

Dagen glanced over but remained quiet. She'd gone from glowers to some indifference. I could live with that. *I won't be here forever.*

The FBI had blocked the street in front of Cherney's house. If there had been an ambulance, it was gone. The men and women in suit jackets and windbreakers studied us with grim faces. One of their own had been injured.

Curious neighbors watched from windows, and one smoked a cigarette on the sidewalk two houses down. A short piece of caution tape ran from a broken fence to a tree beside the house of the neighbor who I'd spoken to about Cherney. Her van was gone.

"Olivia, you're with me. We'll keep the FBI busy. Dagen, with Zach."

I expected a scowl or huff, but Dagen just popped out of the car without a word. The agents watched us but stood as a group when Mika and Olivia approached.

With subtle tugs, I checked for wards as we worked through overgrown brush to the right side of the house. The explosion had emanated from the side of Cherney's house, cracking the window underneath, shredding branches from a tree, and tilting the fence.

The blast had scattered remnants of a router or repeater across the surrounding area. We climbed carefully through the broken slats.

"I don't smell explosive." I lowered my voice. "A blasting ward." From the marks and bent brackets, the center had been the equipment itself.

No other wards lit up. I placed myself where Agent Todd might have, though I had a couple of inches on him.

Did he reach up and touch it? If so, the blast could have been deadly.

Olivia stood behind, watching me.

"Let's see what Cherney might have been connected to."

I turned on the Wi-Fi on my phone and opened the settings, holding my cell up to the edge of the roof. "Can you send these networks to Neddie?"

Without a word, Olivia readied to type.

"Capital L: Linksys-3486; all caps: NETGEAR; 2WIRE199; capital A, R, all one word: AmishRebels."

"This is good. It would be helpful to know all his activities," she said.

Sunrise brightened the eastern sky. We continued to the back, a desolate dry area, checking for wards. The far side proved the easiest to navigate, and Cherney hadn't set any more traps. We stood by his garbage cans, and Olivia tilted the lid open on the recycling bin, but they were both empty.

Dagen struggled into a Kevlar vest with Mika holding both of their suit jackets. I'd never worn one.

The agents had moved to cluster at another car, speaking and watching us with a hint of animosity.

As Olivia and I walked toward Mika, I glanced at the front door, crossed with caution tape. What else have I missed?

I'd sat in a cubicle beside Angel and Izzie for so long, never considering what it was like for the DRCs to be risking their lives. It felt cowardly. My mom's warnings rang through my mind. I could place some of the reason I'd chosen the SDS, and declined the recruitment offer from the DRC, on her words.

"How is Agent Todd?" I asked.

Mika bobbed pink hair to the side. "Not great. Contusions about the head. Lacerations on his face and eyes. He was unconscious when they took him away."

Olivia took Dagen's suit jacket, then Mika's. "I've sent Neddie local Wi-Fi signals and photos of the equipment."

I peeled off my windbreaker and stuffed it between my knees. After a glance around, I placed my holster in the back of the FBI's SUV. The parts of the vest appeared simple, but I followed Mika's example.

"Higher," Dagen grumbled, tapping my shoulder straps.

As I readjusted, my phone dinged, and I paused long enough to read a message from Mom checking on me.

You okay?

Yeah, taking a break.

With the DRC in Reno?

I grimaced.

Yes. Sorry.

Her response took long enough that I almost added an explanation. No need to be sorry. I'm just worried. Not surprised. Call me when you can.

Okay. I wouldn't, not while we searched for Cherney. She wouldn't understand. How had she found out so fast?

"Family?" Mika asked. "You looked uncomfortable."

With a frown, I nodded and finished settling into my vest.

Dagen strapped on her holster and poked at mine. "I take it you practice."

"Every other weekend, most of the time."

Mika dialed on their phone. "Yasmine. You texted about Tim Blanchard's wounds."

With a little jump, Dagen bounced. "Packed sausage."

"I'll let them know." Mika hung up. "Blanchard was bound, magically, when he was stabbed. There's a condition we've seen at wound sites, and Yasmine has confirmed."

As I slid my jacket over vest and holster, Olivia handed me her jacket. "Neddie should be awake. She read my messages, just didn't respond."

"Thanks." Mika started texting, peering up at the cluster of agents. "Olivia, when you're settled, check in with them and set up a liaison. I want a manned car outside of this house."

The vest felt heavy and warm, chafing at the armpit with the holster. *Not quite a sausage*, I thought.

Mika continued, "We've just got a series of reports from Tomas out of Atlanta DRC. He found a link between Cherney and Fahne. Back in 2005, they messaged on 4chan on an arcane discussion board. A short set of back and forth, deleted, but the Consociation archives those routinely. Nothing significant in their conversation, but they were tracked as connected."

The fact that Fahne might be one of Cherney's triad didn't make me any more comfortable about killing him. My thoughts whirled about him, but my chest didn't bottom out like it had earlier.

Olivia darted off to speak with the FBI, and I followed Mika and Dagen back to our vehicle.

"What's next?" Dagen asked.

Mika focused on me. "Thoughts?"

We needed to find Cherney, now, on foot. Neddie might find information on the computers he'd tried to destroy, or his internet activity, but that might be hours later. *Too late.* "His office seems the best bet. He might not have learned about my investigation before he left on Friday, and he called out on Monday. Maybe he has records there that he didn't have time to remove."

THIRTEEN

While we got gas at a bustling station, I picked out some iced tea while Dagen hefted two bags of beef jerky.

"We might get busy. No snacks?" Dagen asked.

"Thanks, no, I'm good." Our exchange came as close to cordial as we'd come.

"Maybe some wheatgrass to chew on." She sniffed and dropped her bags on the counter.

I almost laughed, wondering if her digs meant we were closer, or if I was still the replacement. *Not sure it'll matter once we find Cherney.* Mika purchased my drinks while I waited beside a hot dog roller. From the questionable odor, the food had been there all night.

Ten minutes later, we sat in the parking lot in front of Cherney's contemporary, three-story, brick office with over an hour to wait until they opened. I dug back into the reports.

A report of the disturbance at Devin Gough's residence had only one witness. The woman had called the police from her apartment across the street after a loud boom sounded at 1 a.m. Monday morning. When she looked out, a light was on in a second-floor window, and two dark figures were at the door, breaking in. She was on the phone when they entered, witnessed flashlights downstairs, then saw them arrive to the lit room before racing out of the building. Police responded, finding no sign of Gough but extensive damage in the bedroom. I guessed a blasting ward that Gough had survived somehow.

An attached report mentioned five men arguing in the street a block away at the same time the police checked Gough's apartment. A squad car checked the area an hour later, but found nothing. *Five men?* Cherney, Hilderbrand, Fahne, and Werner were only four; Blanchard was dead by then. Maybe an unrelated group. *Or I'm missing one.*

"Mika?" Olivia gestured to a heavy woman who had parked at the front of the office and juggled a purse and cooler bag.

"Vera was the office manager's name. She fits the description. I love when people get to work early." Mika popped out. "Vera? Agent Mika, FBI."

While the disgruntled office manager waited in her car, we entered the insurance office with me tugging at the realms to make sure Cherney hadn't left any surprises. I even sent a Haven detection spell ahead of us, in case he had retreated here. Vera had been reluctant, but detailed the route to Cherney's upstairs office.

His room surprised me. A picture of three college-aged boys sat prominently on the bookshelf behind his chair, and various framed awards and certificates decorated the walls. He hadn't warded anything, which likely meant he kept nothing here. An air freshener in the wall pumped out a weak, soapy, lavender scent. I expected a closed, dark presence, but Cherney's knickknacks and frivolous mugs made him seem cheery.

"Clear?" asked Mika.

"Yes." I waited as Olivia and Dagen slid into the room. Dagen took the desk and Olivia the rear shelves. Mika trailed behind, sending a lifting spell to tug at a locked file drawer. An unlocking spell followed, working with the lifting spell.

"Bastard," said Dagen from the desk.

We all turned. She had the drawer edged out and pointed inside. It took me a while to spot the wire. Dagen pulled out her phone, turned on the camera, and slid the lip in with the flash on.

Olivia leaned to view the screen. "The line is tied to a detonating cord. The switch is a variant of a number ten. See the glass tube?" She shifted Dagen aside, retrieved a pair of scissors from Cherney's desk, and turned to me. "Please create a small shield, enough to cover my body, but that I can reach around."

"Okay." *Seems we're also the bomb squad.* I pulled a shield from Dur-Alf and formed it between her and the desk and drawer.

She touched it, determining the shape, then reached under and snipped the wire with zero warning or ceremony. I flinched, but she opened the drawer, peering inside. "It hasn't been triggered." With a quick pull, Olivia removed a coil of plastic cord and tucked it into her jacket pocket.

I breathed and released the shield. They obviously had experience in searching someone's office who tried to kill you to hide secrets. I would have yanked that drawer open.

While Mika returned to the filing cabinet, Dagen pulled a satchel from the drawer with care. The zippered plastic container could have been a pen case from my high-school years. On the desk, she opened it in slow stages, as Olivia and I watched. "Smells like charcoal," Dagen said.

Fully opened, I recognized numerous elements that could be used to create arcane sigils: wax, oil, paint and brushes, ink and quills, and charcoal sticks. Nothing that would help us find his location. Sure that the team had come across similar in the past, I felt no need to identify it. Dagen zipped it back up and tossed it into the hall.

We spent the next thirty minutes going through his belongings, my task being relegated to sending photos to Neddie.

"Hello?" Vera called from below.

A male voice murmured.

Mika squeaked a bit of Merfolk, which I guessed to be a curse, and stormed out of the office. "I'll keep them downstairs."

Cherney's calendar showed no events outside of infrequent business meetings, mostly online. Every piece of mail, magazine, or book related to the insurance industry. The knickknacks had no hints of locations, as a souvenir might. The only picture I'd sent that interested me was of his photos. While waiting, I'd checked his background and confirmed that he did not have brothers or sons.

Dagen picked up the kit in the hall. "That's it."

Olivia studied the room, as if reluctant. When her phone rang, she pulled it out and answered, still focused on Cherney's cheery lair. "Agent Nordstrom."

Her eyes whipped to ours, and I hoped for news about Cherney. In the time it took for her to listen, I ran through scenarios where he'd been killed by the two from this morning, picked up on an APB, or at least spotted.

"Thank you." Olivia moved into the hall. "Devin Gough's body has been found crushed in the parking lot of a police station. Reported to the FBI as vehicular homicide, but there are no witnesses. The incident happened at 6:18 a.m., so it's been a while."

A crushing spell. Difficult, but not impossible with arcane sigils. Technically, everything could be recreated, but a lifting spell would be useless unless you had a simple task planned.

We flew down the steps to the lobby, where Mika faced a pale-haired man wearing a sour expression. Vera stood outside.

"Are we done?" he grumbled.

Dagen strode past him wordlessly, head tilted to eye him. Olivia held up her phone to Mika, nodding toward the SUV outside.

Mika clapped the man on the shoulder. "Appreciate the understanding."

He spoke under his breath, but waited until we had all exited before bellowing for Vera in a demanding tone.

"What is it?" Mika asked, heading for the passenger side.

"Devon Gough." Olivia explained the details as she unlocked the car and climbed in.

With the vest, I found the jacket too warm, but wanted to cover the holster. In the confines of the car, my clothes were letting off a bit of a funk.

I'd hoped we'd find Gough alive, and perhaps he'd been heading to the station to report what he'd heard. It would be too much to hope that he was on his way out *after* making a report.

Mika was on the phone, but I asked my question. "Was he leaving the police station?"

Ahead of me, Olivia's head rose. "I think they would have said as much, but I won't assume."

"Good question," said Mika.

Traffic had thickened considerably, and we were traveling along a main road. Mika called and confirmed that Gough hadn't reported to the police, either in person or by phone. I dug through Neddie's reports and sipped my drink while Dagen gnawed on jerky.

We stopped at a light, and Mika twisted about, phone in hand. "Neddie's got a hit on one of the Wi-Fi networks. A direct link to the server you inquired about. Nice call."

Cherney could attempt the same trick, especially without a vehicle and alone. "Can Neddie check incoming requests, not to the more common web searches and such, but to Discord servers or chat rooms? Cherney could be trying to contact others. He might try a burner or hopping off someone's Wi-Fi."

Mika nodded. "If we can track back, we can see what else he's been doing. I like it."

I listened as Mika spoke to Neddie, explaining the idea. "Yeah, I know the load we've got on you. Finding Cherney is front of the line. I'd like it if you dropped us right on top of him."

We still had two men unaccounted for who had run down Werner. They had to be Red Aegis, or they had been hired muscle. Had they just killed Gough?

"We're not going to get Gough's body." Mika turned back to face me. "The police are pitching a fit. I can understand. We just need a quick look at the scene and the damage to confirm it was a crushing spell.

"I want to get some pictures in front of the witnesses who were in the bar when Blanchard was killed. Unless any of you have a better course at the moment."

I shook my head, but guessed we'd find out that Cherney and Hilderbrand had been the ones at the table when Blanchard disturbed them. What could they have said that they'd need to kill him to keep secret?

"I've got a good scent of him now," Dagen said, "if Neddie comes up with any potential locations."

When we pulled into the station, Mika pointed to me

and Dagen. "Walk around the perimeter; they probably have the scene marked off. Olivia and I will take a look at the body and get pictures."

With a forensic team in white, we couldn't miss the spot where Gough had died. An officer tried to wave us away as we approached, but Olivia waved her badge. I at least had a vest with "FBI" that I could sport.

"You're with that group out of Phoenix?" a woman with auburn hair and freckles asked.

"Agent Whelan and Graves." Dagen pointed past the caution tape. "Do you mind? We'll keep well clear."

I could see everything I needed to from where we stood. Amid a bloody stain, the cracked asphalt rippled in a circle, pressured from above and below during the spell. There would be clay shards, if the team hadn't collected them yet.

"Boom," whispered Dagen.

Gough had died two steps from the sidewalk. The attackers could have been on foot or in a car driving down the adjacent road. I couldn't see how this information would help us find Cherney. We sent pictures to Neddie, who responded with a detailed report on the victim.

"I hope your idea pans out. I hate running photos by witnesses. They want to talk." Dagen marched across the parking lot with crisp footsteps.

Sort of a description of an interview. I held my opinion and scrolled through the report on Gough. His friendship with Blanchard included years of social posts at bars, casinos, and on boats. They weren't hiding anything. The two men were witnesses, not Red Aegis, I was sure.

We rounded the corner of the police station, and Dagen headed for the entrance rather than the SUV. I followed, flipping through the report without much interest.

Three officers gathered around the reception desk, and all turned as we came in, interrupting their gossip.

Dagen swaggered toward them, pulling her badge. "Agents Whelan and Graves."

The seated officer said nothing, but put his hand out to receive the badge. He grunted and lifted his hand to me expectantly.

"He's consulting with us. A nerd." She smiled, as if they might find the comment funny.

The man showed no hint of humor. "You can go back inside to your team, but he stays out here."

FOURTEEN

I sat in the police lobby, eyes glazed on a fake palm. *We haven't heard about Agent Todd.* The man had been a bit too bouncy, annoying to some extent. Still, if I'd thought a little more about it, he might not have gotten hurt.

My phone needed charging, so I'd stopped reading Neddie's files. They and the interaction with the team had kept me tethered to the case rather than drifting into painful recollections and dour thoughts. Alone, my mind couldn't help but wander back to the memories of the ghoul and the upcoming funerals. *What if we haven't found Cherney by then?* I wouldn't miss them.

I'm moving. With all the memories, I couldn't stay in that house.

"Wakey-wakey," Dagen called as she marched across the tile of the lobby.

Mika followed, shaking their head. Olivia held evidence bags.

Shoulders tight, I rose. "Anything unexpected?" I asked.

"Not at all," Mika said. "We just had to have their commander dialed up so we could sign out Gough's phone, keys, wallet, and car fob. I want to head to the hotel. Dagen needs an hour on the couch."

"I don't."

"You're getting loopy and whiny."

"You're getting bossy."

"Job description." Mika smiled and addressed me. "Olivia will send you photos. Gough was as crumpled as you might expect."

I lifted my phone. "Need my charger." As they passed for the doors, I followed.

The morning had warmed, especially noticeable in the heavy vest. My mind had to be a little fogged, as it took a moment to realize why everyone waited for me when we approached the car.

Mika cocked their head. "I wasn't concerned, parked in front of Vera, but out here someone might have gotten tricky."

With a crisp march around the car, I checked for wards and clay curse coins. "All clear. Is this normal, having to check the vehicle?" I asked.

Dagen chuckled. "With magic-users, they usually don't see us coming, or they're running."

"She's right." Mika opened the passenger door. "I can identify most wards, unravel some, but I trust your skill at Dur-Alf better than mine. Grateful you're here."

Recruitment pitch? I'd become a bit jaded, and the lack of sleep didn't help.

I hadn't realized how close we were to the hotel until Olivia stopped in a turn lane, earning frantic beeps behind us. I peered through the windshield to see the entrance to the parking lot across the intersection. "Everything okay?" I asked.

"Just being careful," answered Mika.

After annoying a dozen morning commuters, waiting through one light to force the cars following us to go around, we drove across the intersection and entered the parking lot. Olivia parked deep in the lot, leaving us to walk in the sunshine to the entrance of the hotel. The sun warmed us, promising to turn into a hot day.

"Gym bro, did you bring anything other than sweats?" Dagen asked.

That nickname is going to get old. "I didn't think I'd need a suit." I planned on changing in the room and getting out of the vest. My typical work attire was a long-sleeved shirt and slacks. "I brought jeans."

"Doesn't matter," said Mika. "Olivia, follow up with the interviews. I don't trust the Reno police to supply that list, whatever they just said. You might need to drag Neddie into it. I'd like to meet with our first witness by 10 a.m."

Olivia shifted the evidence bags to her other arm, where she carried a black travel case, and I reached out, offering to help. She stopped, handing me the load.

"What's in the case?" I asked. The size of a lunch cooler, it had a hard shell under the fabric.

"Electronics. We can attempt to connect Neddie to Gough's cell remotely." She entered the number on her phone, and I focused on the items in the evidence bags.

Blood had crusted everything, and the shattered screen of the cell gave me little hope of finding anything. The man had died brutally.

"Did you expect this from the Red Aegis?" Mika had noted my expression, and I softened it.

"We've known their ideals, but beyond some early activities with Tarus, they've quieted. I assumed recruiting. But yes, their actions about a decade ago were brutal."

"Three malls, if I remember correctly."

"Two in Europe and one in Brazil. Seventeen dead. The Consociation is still cleaning up the mess. Rumors keep leaking out. The DRCs at the time ended up killing five of the members, which is when we learned about their organization." With hundreds of downloads from Cherney's server alone, who knew what we could expect.

"Then they went quiet," Mika stated.

"Very quiet." In the five years that I'd worked for the SDS, only a dozen leads had come into the office about the Red Aegis, and none had led to anything, until Cherney.

We entered the hotel, where the air held the aroma of breakfast. A new shift of attendants at the counter glanced up, then continued their conversation as we made for the elevators. Olivia lagged behind us, speaking with a patient tone, though it sounded like they'd been hopping her from one department to the next.

Dagen swiped the door key before I even thought of checking for wards. I tugged at the realms belatedly, but nothing showed. She strode through, red hair bobbing in a shrug. "Fine, I'll take a quick nap."

Mika glanced at me. "You could use one."

I hefted the bags. "I can help. I'm okay with tech."

"Okay. Grab a rinse and fresh clothes. You might not get another chance."

As I opened my mouth to say I didn't need a shower, Dagen faced me, rubbing her nose. "You stink."

My funk had been noticeable, but hardly that bad. *Unless you had keen scent.* Without a word, I knelt by my case, grabbing a change of clothes. The day was only going to get hotter.

I left the vest and my holstered gun on the kitchen counter and closed myself in the bathroom. Olivia spoke in the living room, repeating witness names, numbers, and addresses to someone in the police department. Some of that information had been in the reports, but not all.

My stubble hadn't grown out much, and I had left my trimmer at the house anyway. I stripped, wadding clothes near the door, and brushed my teeth while the shower steamed the room. These moments by myself proved to be the worst. My jellyfish tattoo reminded me of Peter's, which led to Beth's sleeves. Splashes of cold water on my face broke some of the memories before I moved under the fog and steaming spray.

Ten minutes later, I exited wearing a subtle Slipknot T-shirt that the vest would cover. Dagen had disappeared into a bedroom, and the others didn't comment on it.

Mika rested on the couch, phone in hand, and Olivia worked on Gough's cell at the dining room table.

"We've got confirmation from Yasmine on Hilderbrand's death. He must have been bound when someone painted an oil sigil on his throat. Crushing spell." Mika looked up. "Feel better?"

Haunted. "Yes." I stuffed my dirty clothes in my case before wandering toward Olivia.

On bloodied napkins, she had a line hooked up to the port of the damaged phone, connected to a small black box with a screen that could have been a Wi-Fi hotspot. The back cover of Gough's cell had been removed. Her phone lay at her right hand, and she responded to someone's texts. I hovered at her shoulder.

"Phone's active, but the battery has cut out twice. Neddie's gone through the data folder and says there's a draft text." Olivia typed as she spoke.

At the mention of battery, I moved to my backpack and jacked my charger into the kitchen.

"Here's the text." Olivia read, facing Mika, who listened. "I'm afraid to text you. They are aliens, and I know it. You'll think I'm nuts, but they killed Tim. With a touch, they froze him in the middle of a sentence, then stabbed him. They didn't care that I was sitting at the table.

"Didn't care.

"I know. Crazy.

"I swear it's true. They are hunting me. They have to be aliens. Who else could freeze a person?

"If I send you this, they'll hunt you. If I go to the police, they won't believe me.

"Before they killed him, Tim told me he had heard them say something about a stampede, and then they gave him a weird look. Stampede. What does that mean?

"I'm writing this behind a laundromat. I'm afraid to go home. You'll think I'm nuts if I send this to you.

"I've read this and don't dare send it.

"I'm turning my phone off for now. They'll be tracking it." Olivia finished, turning to Mika, then me. "Stampede?" she asked.

It made no sense to me. Nothing from the realms stampeded, that I'd ever heard of, so I waited for Mika or Olivia to continue.

"I'd guess that we're losing something in the translation," Mika said. "Whatever Tim Blanchard heard, and repeated, might not be stampede. I'm sure of the meaning, and don't see any relevance."

"None worth killing someone over," I agreed, frowning at the phone.

"It's half-past eight." Mika pointed me to the room behind me. "The waitress who was serving that evening will be in at 10:30 to serve lunch today. Grab a quiet hour, sleep, or read reports, unless you've got a better idea. I'm going to meditate."

Alone time wasn't my best scenario, but I stepped into

the dark and forced myself to lie down. From the reports, I'd always assumed the DRC to be more on the go, or at least on stakeouts. I rested back on the covers. My eyes were dry and welcomed closing.

I woke to a rap on the open door. "Up. We've got an issue at the insurance agency. Someone triggered a ward or something. Vera said that jerk was in the file room soon after we left." Mika bit off the last sentence with a sharp, annoyed tone.

"When?" I threw my feet to the floor, blinking. "When did this happen?"

"A while ago. She finally remembered to call me. Bomb disposal has been ordered by the police."

What had Cherney been hiding?

CHAPTER

FIFTEEN

"Was it the man you were talking to?" I asked. "In the lobby of Cherney's building?"

Dagen fussed as she pulled on her vest, Velcro tangling in her red hair, so I moved to mine.

Mika nodded. "Stroupe. He played it up that he was a senior something and needed more details. I should have guessed he'd go snooping."

"How bad is he hurt?"

"Tore up his right arm. Vera left and called me when she got to a bar, from the sounds of the background noise. She might have already been drinking."

Olivia waited at the table where the contents of Gough's wallet had been spread out.

I cinched my holster over the vest and grabbed my phone. Dagen pointed to my windbreaker. "Cover up, cowboy. This isn't the wild west."

"Yeah." I didn't relish wearing all of this in the summer heat, and from Mika's impatient expression, I grabbed my half-full water bottle without taking the time to top it off.

We jogged down the halls, drawing surprised attention from a couple exiting their room. The lobby had grown busier, but not by much, and they too paused as we raced through.

When I checked, the SUV hadn't been warded, so we piled in, and I had a moment to focus as we drove. Hours before, Cherney had left the parking lot where his partner, Werner, had been killed. Since no one had said otherwise, they hadn't seen him or picked him up. *He might be long gone.* The thought reignited yesterday's anger, and I tensed. I preferred to continue with the plan of using me as bait rather than search his office.

"Agent Todd is out of surgery," Olivia said as she turned at an intersection. "He's blind in one eye and still unconscious, but they believe he will survive."

I winced. A hefty price to pay. His puppy-like cheerfulness didn't deserve that consequence. "Do we have any data of Cherney's activities through the piggybacked network?" Some results would make Agent Todd's sacrifice more meaningful.

"Too much." Mika twisted to face me and brushed aside a pink strand. "He managed four websites, including the one you tracked. They've been locked down, but the downloads are kicking the Consociation into alert. The rituals being distributed are designed to open both Tarus and Ya-Keya."

Dagen cursed. "So there will be a bunch of unwitting transitions of people who won't know how to handle being a werewolf. No biera to guide them."

"Biera? The term is familiar." Something I'd read ages ago.

Dagen huffed. "A group of werewolves who mentor during transition. I thought you were the smart one?"

"Thanks."

She smiled at my reply.

"So," continued Mika, "we've got our hands full tracking downloads. Neddie promises to see where the myriad chatroom connections lead. There was one login to one of Cherney's websites since he left his house. It came from a burner phone at the Phoenix airport. We've got it tagged, but it's shut off."

Halfway through Mika's comment, my hope rose, but dropped by the end. A cell we could track would be too much to ask. "Do we know what changes he made to the website he logged into?" I asked.

"No." Mika settled forward in the seat, pulling up their phone. "I'll see if we can find out."

I stared out my window, letting the cars and sides of the road blur. We could eliminate Blanchard and Gough from the Red Aegis as innocent bystanders. On top of Cherney, we had the two who had run down Werner on the loose. *The numbers don't add up.* I spoke aloud, pondering. "What if we have two triads here?"

Mika turned around again. "Explain."

"We've got six in play, at minimum. Cherney is alive. So are the two who killed Werner. Fahne. Hilderbrand. One of the second triad could have been Cherney's contact. Perhaps there's an argument, if that's an appropriate term, over Cherney's activities."

Olivia spoke. "That is more logical than assuming they would hire people."

"It is," agreed Mika.

The argument would have to be significant, to warrant killing each other. Had Cherney or one of the others broken some internal rule? *Peter and Beth.* Had their deaths been the start of this feud? A cold part of me did not believe enough Red Aegis had died, if that were the case.

When we arrived at the insurance office, the police had

seven squad cars blocking the area. Red and blue lights reflected off the brick and glass while onlookers huddled in the shade of a building across the street. An angry officer tried to wave off Olivia, then swore when Mika dangled a badge out of the window.

With a shout, he called a barrel of a man from one of the cars. By the time we'd parked and climbed out, an officer charged us like a bull, picking me to yell at. "You the FBI who cleared this building this morning?"

"We were," said Mika coolly.

He turned, then blinked, as if seeing Mika for the first time. His eyes darted from the pink hair, to the suit, to the vest, ending with the badge. "You in charge?"

"Agent Mika. Nordstrom, Whelan, and Graves. Have you secured the building perimeter?"

"I got a man on the back door."

"That's very good, thank you. You've called bomb squad, I assume?" Mika asked, knowing that the unit had been called. "Excellent. You've got this well in hand."

He flustered, lips opening and tapping closed, before he managed a weak comment. "One of the workers was seriously injured this morning."

"That's unfortunate. Do you know whether the file room is upstairs or downstairs?" Mika had the man off balance.

Mika did this with me, when I'd been angry. The revelation made me feel somewhat manipulated, but I respected the skill as well.

"Downstairs, but you can't go in there."

Mika produced a card, handing it to the officer. "We're a tactical unit. Trained. Here is my supervisor, Isaac. Give him a call."

Olivia tapped my elbow, and the dark cloud of Tarus swirled about her as she stepped past. I took the hint and followed her while the squat, distracted officer stared at the card.

Mika spoke in a quiet tone, engaging who I guessed to be the ranking officer. Other police between us and the building had been watching, and since it seemed we'd just left with permission, they didn't stop us.

As we stepped inside, the acrid tang of blood hung in the air. Dark droplets led the way. I tugged at the realms out of caution, repeating the action as we headed for the file room. A row of fluorescent lights hung over the rectangular space where shelves lined all the walls. To the right, shreds of spattered paper and cardboard littered the confines, but no wards glowed.

"I don't see anything," I told Olivia as she pulled out a flashlight.

She slid past me, illuminating the remaining banker boxes and a bowed metal shelf. "Do you smell any explosives?"

"No." Stroupe had left one box on the floor, lid askew. I knelt, digging through the files, before moving to the confetti strewn about.

Olivia's phone buzzed, and she pulled it out, putting it on speaker on a shelf. "Mika?"

"We've got a nice standoff going. What do you have in there?"

I found the top corner of a bank statement and flipped it over.

"One box exploded, and neither of us smells explosives, so it was likely a magical ward. I'm still checking the surrounding boxes for trip wires. Zach, can you set a shield for me?"

The information at the top of my page did not have Cherney's information, but detailed a business account of Matt Fahne's.

"Yes. I just found Fahne's bank statement. Why would Cherney have that?" I stood.

"Interesting," Mika said.

With a step back, Olivia motioned to a box. "Can you contain it, then jostle it to the side? It will help determine if there's a motion charge and give me access to the box behind it."

Here's to something new. I wrapped the box in a shield, at least all but the bottom sitting on the shelf, and overlapped extra between us and the potential detonation. With a brief hesitation, I pulled a lifting spell and with a rough shove, jerked it to an empty space like it contained a wasps' nest. Nothing exploded. My breath whistled past my lips, and I realized I'd been holding it in.

"Thanks." Olivia shone her flashlight into the hand opening of the back box.

"All good?" asked Mika.

"All good." *A new line on my resume.* I returned to the shreds on the floor, digging out a torn strip larger than the others. "This piece of paper has a printout of Jay Werner's phone records. December of last year."

"Doxing his partners?" Mika sounded amused.

"If so, it won't be particularly helpful to us. I think the box was at the back of the shelf."

"I believe so," Olivia agreed. "I've got six total with Cherney's name on them. What do you suppose Stroupe, maybe his supervisor, was digging around for?"

I pulled out two more readable pieces from the confetti, both with itemized bank statements, but not a section I could assign to anyone. "He might have thought that we were searching for something that might be stolen or valuable. What did you tell Stroupe, Mika?"

"That we needed Cherney's location. That he was a

witness we needed to locate. The usual. People don't usually believe it. How much is salvageable?"

With my sneaker, I swept aside the shreds I stood on. "The blast was pretty thorough. I'm surprised I haven't found a finger. You might be able to piece together some of these fragments, but we could likely recreate the documents easier. Bank statements. Phone records."

"See if you can find a garbage bag. Neddie should be able to do something with them."

No wonder she was so grumpy. I stood, checking Olivia's progress as she teased open a cardboard box with her flashlight. "I'll be right back."

It took longer than expected to find a large black bag in the cupboard of a tiny kitchenette. Olivia waited for me to move another box.

"Anything interesting in them?" I noted the first file container on top of the one on the floor.

"Records, as labeled." She pointed to the front box at the edge of the shelf, and I shielded it and moved it with less drama.

Mika's voice came through the speaker. "I've got a report from Neddie on Cherney's website activity. He deleted spam."

"A comment marked as spam?" I clarified.

"Yes."

"Did we retrieve it?"

"Yes. In the report. It's spam."

A grin tugged at my lips. "Can we bother Neddie to pull up the deleted spam comments for the past few months or year? They might be messages."

"New to me." Mika sniffed. "Will do."

Once I got started filling the bag, I headed back to find a broom and made quick work of the floor around Olivia.

"Okay," Mika said, stretching the word out, "we've got bomb squad pulling up. Almost done?"

"Yes. About ninety seconds," answered Olivia, digging through file folders.

I tossed the bag of scraps over my shoulder and left the broom against a shelf. Blood smeared the floor. I hadn't looked too hard for body parts.

When I followed Olivia out, past the first glaring policewoman, a tiny clay disk shattered on the concrete five feet from my side.

CHAPTER

SIXTEEN

The blast shredded my garbage bag. Confetti plumed over my head. My ears rang.

Out beside the cars, two more explosions shattered windows and dented doors.

I'd been pushed to one knee from the detonation; three feet closer and I might have been wounded. I stood, drawing my weapon.

The police were doing the same, but while they searched the street, I aimed up, searching from where the curse coin had been dropped. The brick wall rose to a sharp edge, with no gutter on a flat roof. The stylized building had a section over the lobby only one floor high and a higher area three stories tall. I guessed our attacker would be hiding at the top and trained my weapon there.

A handful of clay coins rained over the edge, toppling against the blue sky.

With both hands on my Glock, it took me too long to pull a shield. I flashed Dur-Alf green over Olivia's black hair, close enough that it flattened one strand. Spread wide, the shield encompassed us and the shoulder of the officer at the front door.

Magical blasts lack any heat, just a sudden expulsion of force. As the first chips cracked against the concrete, the gusts they produced both threw some coins away from us and activated others in midair.

My knees buckled from the pressure. The world echoed in a silent whine.

The officer we'd been passing, a stout woman, caught a spray of thunderclaps that ripped her weapon out of her hand, scraped her face, and pummeled her back toward the doors that shattered. In my vision, these were flashes of dark green from Dur-Alf.

In the eight yards between us and the parked cars, three clustered policemen took blasts at their ankles. They all went down to the sandstone-painted cement, one with a badly turned knee that might have had a protruding tibia or fibula. As it bounced against the ground, a weapon discharged with an orange flash and smoke, though I couldn't hear it.

A pair of clay tokens broke at the bumpers of the closest parked cars, shattering headlights.

When the mayhem subsided to anguished men, I had rolled to my side, back to the entrance, still clutching the Glock. Olivia knelt beside me, twin cuts under one cheekbone. She grabbed my shoulder, darkening the blue sky with Tarus, and pulled me up. I'm an inch short of six feet and one-hundred-seventy pounds, so the strength in her slight frame surprised me.

Mika and Dagen were gone, the SUV doors left open.

Four officers were belatedly popping out of their cars like prairie dogs with weapons that they aimed in seemingly random, confused patterns.

I tossed a Haven detection spell to the roof above, lighting us all with ghostly white. *Weak.* Through it, a faint glimpse of movement reached the far side of the building and hopped down about five feet, then did so again as if there were giant steps there. *Cherney.* As I sprang into a run, ahead, I caught the wispy trails of Mika and Dagen racing toward our attacker.

Olivia passed me in a flash, reaching the corner of the building to turn out of my sight before trailing as a white Haven ghost. Past the brick, I could see the heavier shape of Dagen leaping toward her prey, only to fall stiff to the ground. Bound?

Mika, thinner in form, but a hair taller, stopped two steps away from Dagen. Our pursuit had disappeared from the range of my weak Haven spell.

As I reached the rear parking lot, gun raised to fire, Fahne's dead face flashed in my memory, and I nearly stumbled. My pulse, already pounding, skipped, and my chest tightened.

As I raced through empty parking spaces by the building, Olivia stood firing one-handed to her left toward a stone wall that enclosed the lot. Two-story apartments rose on the other side, but I could see no one, except Dagen, bound straight ahead of me at the foot of a tall Ponderosa Pine.

A stride away, blood pulsed silently from Olivia's left shoulder, but she kept firing. *Hell.* The enforced quiet made the sight more disturbing.

I shifted my weapon's aim to hers, but also drew a binding spell from Dur-Alf. Coins scattered along the asphalt glowed green. *Didn't even see those.*

Across the road, a short metal fence marked a parking lot; farther down the street was the next entrance for a development of white, clay-topped apartments. From that area, behind the cover of the sparse fence and a thin tree, two men fired, retreating step-by-step. Dressed in pale Hawaiian shirts and wearing pastel shorts, they appeared more like tourists, except for the muzzle flashes.

At a hundred and fifty feet away, I could more likely hit them with a bullet than a binding spell.

After the memory of Fahne, I threw the spell.

The benefit of a spell against mundanes, even arcanists, is that they can't see it coming. As the binding closed in, I grew confident, then three things happened. When my spell hit the pale man with the graying goatee, he flashed the mossy-green of Dur-Alf, and my binding slipped off. Second, something invisible tackled him. *Mika.*

Third, the man's partner planted a bullet into the vest I wore, punching my rib cage where it ended on my right side. I staggered and pushed my gun hand there. My focus remained on Mika's invisible tackle of the shooter and the other who raced away, no longer firing.

I sucked in air and stopped in pain. My eyes trailed after the Red Aegis attacker we were losing as he raced from us.

Olivia waved her good arm to catch my attention, weapon holstered. Her mouth moved, but I shook my head. *Deaf. Permanent?* That thought left a hollow in my chest. *My music.*

She indicated Dagen, and I nodded, checking on Mika, who had wrapped the man tight in a lifting spell. An ineffective binding, but workable.

Behind me, Olivia trailed blood. I pointed out the clay coins. Dagen had likely stepped on one of the land mines. Each step and movement of my arm awakened the bruise on my ribs. As I tugged loose the Dur-Alf binding on Dagen, shields at the corner lit. As she spun to her feet, spitting out muted words, I kept tugging on the realm as I walked toward the far side of the building.

A series of seven shields had been placed like steps that led from the roof, along the wall to the ground, and spanned ten yards in their descent. *Ingenious.*

It took a moment before I spotted the fresh chunks of red clay spattered on the stairs, then the fresh bullet holes in the wall above.

Dagen had left to help Mika, as we all should have, probably, but the mystery intrigued me. I turned to Olivia, who peered at the brick shards. To her, they'd be floating in the air. Her deltoid muscle had been ripped open. She appeared careful not to move it.

With a wince at my ribs, I holstered my weapon, checked on Mika and Dagen, and pulled out my cell. With it, I gestured toward my ear. "Deaf."

My text to her said the same.

DEAF. ARE YOU OKAY?

She read the message, shrugged, and gestured toward the brick pieces on the shield.

I took pictures of the shards, zooming in on the bullet holes, then pointed to where the shooters had been standing. "Fired from there."

Behind her, a trio of officers had swarmed onto our side of the parking lot, but they moved in a slow, confused jumble. Deft with Mer lifting spells, I used two and began picking up clay coins from their path. *Last thing we need to explain after this.* When one noticed movement, I tumbled them like leaves toward us, though the movement countered the breeze.

The group studied us, weapons drawn though pointed down as they stalked bewildered through the empty lot. They appeared relieved when they spotted Mika, now visible, and Dagen securing a prisoner.

Tucked in a shield, I blasted the assemblage of coins, a mix of blasts and bindings. The trio of officers jogged toward Mika and Dagen. I tugged the stairs loose, then texted Olivia.

I THINK THAT THOSE TWO WERE FIRING AT THE ONE ON THE ROOF WHEN HE ESCAPED.

Mika would have seen his glow in Haven from my detection spell, and Dagen had followed the lead.

MIKA LIKELY SAW IT, I added.

With that comment, we ambled toward the rest of the DRC. I dearly wanted to remove the vest and its pressure against my ribs, but no one else had. Olivia's heavy bleeding had stopped. *She's tough.* If I'd had her wound, I'd be lying down waiting for the ambulance.

Mika had borrowed zip cuffs from one of the three officers, and everyone appeared to be talking at once. They glanced at us, then focused on Olivia's arm, and whatever argument they'd been in the middle of seemed to fizzle.

With a flash of a smile to us, Mika began talking on their phone. Dagen approached me, leaning in to speak in my ear.

I scoffed and pointed. "Deaf."

She rolled her eyes, said something derisive based on the quirk of her lips, then pinched her fingers together.

A binding spell?

The officers had pulled back to the street, meeting with a fourth, so I leaned in and whispered, "Binding spell?"

Dagen pulled back, motioning with her hand to keep my voice down, then nodded. I complied and bound the prisoner with Dur-Alf.

Our attacker turned captive had graying hair and a deadpan expression. He sported a well-trimmed goatee on cheeks that had been freshly shaved. *Who are you in this?*

We'd been ambushed, possibly by Cherney, who had in turn been taken by surprise. A rival triad? I'd have preferred catching Cherney, but this man might give us some insight into the goings-on over the past couple of days. *Which one had made the trap?* Did I still want revenge over Peter and Beth? Yes, a part of me did.

I rubbed my ear, then winced. It hurt. If I lost my hearing, a large part of my life would disappear; playing with William and the band, all my music.

Would I still have tracked my partners' murderers if I'd known the consequence? *Yes.*

Dagen studied my hair with an impish smile.

"What?" I asked.

She shrugged, turning to hide her expression.

I scrubbed fingers through my scalp, and bits of white confetti flowed out of it. *That garbage bag of shredded paper.*

CHAPTER
SEVENTEEN

I stood in the ringing silence as Dagen and Olivia spoke from beside the bound man. Fear of losing my hearing tugged at the edge of my mind, and I rubbed the short stubble on my face, trying to divert the thoughts. The Consociation had access to magical healing, so I'd wait until they tried to help me before I panicked.

Where we stood, we blocked a curving drive into an apartment complex, and while the police had cordoned off the insurance building, the street was open. A car pulled up the road, slowing, and I tensed, but the woman appeared to want to turn. *Not a good idea*, I thought. After a solid study of the man bound on the asphalt, she pulled away.

Across the way, a pair of officers watched us. On the far side of the building, strobing lights flashed, likely from ambulances attending to the wounded. I'd barely glimpsed the damage that the curse coins had caused, but the police had been hurt. I still took shallow breaths, avoiding the worst stabs of pain from my ribs.

My phone buzzed in my hand. Mika texted, so I turned to them before reading.

HELP ON THE WAY. HOLD TIGHT.

I gave her a shrug, then typed.

THANK YOU. DO WE HAVE AN ID?

I pointed at the man.

NEDDIE HAS PHOTOS. WORKING ON IT.

I gestured down the side road to the main intersection

CHERNEY?

Mika frowned before they answered.

DIDN'T GET A GOOD LOOK. I THINK SO. USED SHIELDS TO GET DOWN WITH HIS BACK TO ME. HE RAN FOR THE STREET, BUT THESE TWO WERE SHOOTING.

WHY? ANY IDEA?

I'M HOPING OUR CAPTIVE WILL HAVE SOMETHING TO SAY ABOUT IT.

I wasn't as hopeful. Fanatics tended to keep pretty closed-mouthed.

WE CAN HOPE, I replied.

Mika's smile grew as they typed.

LILY.

I glanced from my phone to Mika, tilting my head. *Was this supposed to mean something?*

A FLOWER?

A DRAGON-SHIFTER. THE RED AEGIS ARE ON ELEVATED STATUS SINCE THEY ARE LINKED TO THE OPENING OF TARUS. LILY CAN INTERROGATE HIM AND SHE'S BOARDING A FLIGHT FROM PHOENIX.

I knew a little of dragon-shifter abilities, but I'd considered their skill of magically forcing people to speak the truth as little more than gossip. Mika didn't appear to think so, and why else fly one here?

As I digested meeting a dragon-shifter up close, Mika texted.

DID YOU HAVE TROUBLE GETTING A BINDING ON HIM?

I nodded.

Mika pulled at Mer, but nothing showed.

With no expectations, I tugged at Dur-Alf, and almost missed it. A pale green glow at his collar. We both saw it. *A binder's block.* I also spotted two coins in the grass by the fence ten feet away. I pointed and prepared a shield and blasting spell to destroy the clay curse tablets.

As Mika leaned to inspect the gray-haired man, I destroyed the coins, then spoke, though I could only feel my words rumble in my bones. "A binder's block. The ward reacts to Dur-Alf." Dwarves were notorious for using them.

Mika cocked their head and rolled a spinning finger at the binding I had on the man, as if wondering how I'd managed to affix the spell.

"Ineffective up close." I leaned forward. "I can pull the ward apart."

When Mika lifted the flowered collar of the Hawaiian shirt, it exposed a thin strip of beige paper somehow attached to the neckline; the piece tore.

The midnight realm of Tarus plumed into existence, billowing from the man's chin.

My surprise took precious seconds as I blinked.

Six feet from where I stood, the opening to the realm expanded upward from our captive's head. Like a startled cat, Mika sprang back.

Dagen, unaware of the danger but recognizing Mika's concern, leaped forward, claws protruding.

My hand went to my weapon, but I did not have the team's ammo that would affect any serious, long-lasting damage on a demon or other cryptid of Tarus. My pulse sped as I reached to my left side, tugging a binding spell from Dur-Alf. A rift in a realm would soon close, but only after something emerged from it, and I knew of no way to seal it; I could only prepare for what might materialize.

Partly hidden, the prisoner's body jerked. With my binding in place, it could not have been of his own accord.

Out of the midnight fog of Tarus, a gray hand the size of my head swung. Skinless muscles rippled as they moved with reddish creases and lines. Stubby dark nails protruded from fingers and tore into Dagen's vest.

The impact spun her, but she managed a rake of her own claws across the draugr's forearm before she toppled away from us. Black oozed from the cryptid's wounds.

In the blink of an eye, a second arm darted out, then a head, roughly human-shaped, with black eyes and wet muscles and tendons stretched over cheek and jaw. Dark teeth lined the lipless mouth.

With arms outstretched, the draugr sprung at Mika as its gruesome body ejected from the dark realm like a sprung coil.

I moved with a frustrating slowness, almost throwing the binding before pulling back, fearful that I might catch Mika in it instead.

One-handed, Olivia ripped into the side of the cryptid, darting between me and the others. I took one step back, jaw set, with my spell readied.

Mika rolled from under the grasp of the distracted draugr, and Olivia bounded out of the cryptid's reach as it attempted to retaliate against her attack. I noted her eyes snatching a glance at me.

They'd left me primed to attack. The cryptid, untangled from both of them, pivoted its black pits of eyes toward me, its leg muscles sliding against each other as it turned.

The moment reminded me of the ghoul in the tent with Beth's torn body. I could feel the raging yell as it coursed through me. Spell in my palm, I slammed it toward the swinging claws.

We met, and the cryptid's nails ripped into the pads of my fingers and palm, one piercing spike protruding through the back of my hand between thumb and forefinger. At the same moment, my binding slapped into the almost human fingers, wrapping around the body like a snake. As the world around me appeared to slow, I thought of my music, my guitar, and my hand.

The draugr fell stiff, driven by momentum, and its nails ripped free of my flesh. It toppled against the legs of our prisoner. The opening to the realm had cleared. As my eyes followed, it took a second glance to confirm that the man's head was gone. Shreds of tendons from the neck hinted at the violence, but the rest had disappeared into Tarus.

The muzzle flash of Mika's weapon preceded a dull noise against the ringing in my ears. *Not deaf.*

The draugr's head exploded, painting the asphalt with a black gelatin.

My left knee buckled, but I held my stance. Pain ebbed up my arm from my bloody hand.

Mika touched Mer, and illusions covered the draugr and man. The cryptid faded from sight, and the man appeared as he had been when alive. A lifting spell whipped at my hand, spinning around it and tightening to quell the bleeding.

Olivia moved with a careful step around the illusion she couldn't see. With one hand on my shoulder, she moved me toward the short fence and leaned me against it.

Dagen had rebounded and stood beside Mika on their phone. They both glanced toward the insurance office, so I turned there, dazed. *I survived two cryptids out of Tarus.* Most witches died of old age without seeing one. *Except for those who work for the DRC.*

A pair of officers jogged toward us, weapons drawn.

They saw the draugr. A whole department of the Consociation dealt with cases such as theirs, scrubbing the truth from existence or at least burying it from prying eyes. How, I didn't know, but the mundanes could not learn of the cryptids without causing worldwide panic.

As Mika moved to intercept the police, Dagen retrieved my phone from the asphalt. I hadn't even known I'd dropped it. Her vest had deep shreds in it, and one appeared wet. *So quick.* In one short period of time, we'd been wounded, Olivia the worst, and lost both Cherney and one other Red Aegis.

From her smirk, Dagen said something she considered funny, or disparaging, before pacing back toward Mika's illusion.

Olivia moved to position her good arm toward me and sat on the ground against the fence, motioning me to do the same. I complied, sliding so as not to fall. The ache in my ribs complained, but I didn't consider taking off the soaked vest anymore. My hand bled a little, despite the wraps of Mer wound about it. I resisted flexing it. *No guitar for a while.*

The FBI arrived, and I recognized one of the women who pulled into the drive, blocking it. Mika and Dagen spoke with them, keeping everyone clear of the illusion that wrapped the human and cryptid corpses.

The man had been fanatical enough to booby trap his own clothing with Tarus. *His own body.* I couldn't imagine it. The Red Aegis wanted to expose the Consociation to the mundanes, and I could see their reasoning, but their means baffled me.

My eyes widened, and I turned to Olivia. "Yasmine. Tarus in the clothes." Someone had to warn her.

Olivia attempted a comforting smile, but it appeared as

an awkward, strained expression. She pantomimed a phone call, followed by a pointed finger at Mika.

"Mika already warned her," I confirmed.

With a nod, Olivia relaxed her face to its normal studious deadpan and alert eyes.

A cluster of people had gathered at cars in the parking lot of the apartments. A trail of smoke or vape highlighted them leaning against a sedan in the full sun. The temperature had risen above comfortable toward hot, especially in the vest. A faint whiff of the dead shifted in the light breeze.

I tensed as a pink and white antique tank of a car pulled down the asphalt from the direction of the apartments. Some cars had started down that drive, seen us blocking it at the end, and backed up, but this one continued toward us. Olivia waved her hand at me in dismissal, and in a moment, Dagen and Mika left the FBI to greet the newcomer.

The black man who exited wore a cowboy hat and boots that matched stylishly with a gray Guayabera shirt and tight jeans. He had a strong, affable smile as he greeted them and flicked a glance at us before reaching into the back seat for a bag. I would have asked Olivia who he was, but we'd end up texting, and I didn't want to move. The three of them left his car door open as they marched toward us. Dagen pointed at the wet gouge in her vest.

"Dwarf?" I asked Olivia. In the Consociation, they were the most proficient healers. Merfolk were close behind.

She gave me a tight nod in confirmation.

As Mika and Dagen spoke, they paused for a moment at the corpses, then the man, or the illusion of a handsome human, knelt in front of Olivia and me. He spoke to both of us, but I just stared flatly. From his bag, he produced a fruit juice pouch and plunged the straw into it before handing it to Olivia. She took it readily and began drinking. *Blood?*

He crouched oddly as he reached toward her shoulder, not quite touching. I tried to imagine the dwarf inside the illusion.

Even as he worked on Olivia, his left hand wiggled fingers at me. A cold, uncomfortable ache washed over me, like plunging into ice water, more so, the stiff shock it produced. My head, ribs, and hand were the epicenters, but the effect coursed through me.

I gritted my teeth, willing my hearing to come back. My breathing became forced and ragged from the exertion of the healing against my body and my concern.

". . . out here," he was saying. "I mean, the water is fabulous this time of year. Let's hope you wrap this up before I get sent somewhere." He focused on me. "Better?"

My throat tightened. I'd lost so much, and my music might be the only thing left to keep me sane. "Beautiful," I said.

"Thanks. Though, I meant your hearing. You might end up with tinnitus. Hard to tell."

I laughed, with a pang of guilt, but smiled. "Thank you, yes, better."

CHAPTER

EIGHTEEN

At Everek's insistence, I remained sitting as he had Dagen lie on the asphalt for her healing.

Olivia rested beside me, draining a second pouch.

"Did we send pictures of the man, before?" I nudged a chin toward the illusion, which depicted the gray-haired head.

She pulled her lips off the straw. "Yes. Neddie has them."

Everek glanced at the street between us and the insurance company. "Yasmine's going to need a place to pull in, Mika," he called over his shoulder. I hadn't seen him on his phone.

As we waited for Mika to disengage with one of the FBI, I asked, "How do you know where Yasmine is?"

He pointed to his illusion's head. "Comms. Mika avoids them, but it works for Yasmine, Neddie, and me. A lot of chatter goes on while you're out gunslinging."

"Gym bro froze," said Dagen. "Didn't take his shot."

I considered the choice to use the spell before the

weapon. The gray-haired man's block had foiled my binding, but the decision had still been correct. "Might not want to fling around the term 'froze' considering where you were during all this."

She surprised me by laughing. "Good point. Not all muscle from the neck up, are you?"

Everek glanced between us. "Dagen, I thought you were pissed at this guy, from what Yasmine said."

"Oh, I'd rather have someone qualified. Don't get me wrong. A witch with some experience, if they're going to replace Phistrel. But he's okay, if he doesn't keep freezing."

"I don't need Wild Bill Hickok," said Mika, approaching. "Zach's here for his analytical ability. Olivia has proved time and again that brains will get us there."

Dagen's slowly warming attitude toward me and Mika's compliment appeared genuine, but I did not feel part of the team. *Why hadn't they just locked me away until they'd secured Cherney?*

"Mika, need the FBI to clear the drive for Yasmine." Everek tipped his hat. "When you get a chance."

"Got it. Olivia, give Zach the keys. I'd like to pull our ride over where we can see it." Mika nodded. "Check it. I wouldn't put it past Cherney to circle around."

I rose, reaching for the keys Olivia dug out. Her shoulder hadn't been bandaged yet, and the dried blood had caked on her skin and jacket.

Since Mika paused, waiting for me, I joined them. "Any thoughts on a next step?" they asked.

"Learn how Cherney got here to ambush us. I'd have thought he'd book."

Mika nodded, but didn't reply.

"Can Dagen scent him?" I pointed down the street to the intersection. "Maybe we find he's on foot, or he parked nearby. If so, someone might have seen it. Getting a description of his vehicle might help."

"Good." Mika flashed a smile and veered off toward the FBI blocking the drive.

I'd grown accustomed to their easy nature, quick smiles, and compliments, but I didn't trust that Mika wasn't manipulating me. *For what?* They had my case files on the Red Aegis.

I kept pace and asked, "Why did you let me join the investigation?"

With a glance over their shoulder for a brief scrutiny of my expression, Mika turned to face the FBI as we walked and answered. "One. I wanted you on the team years ago. Two. I would have had to lock you up to keep you from investigating. Three. Your psych eval doesn't make me believe you'll go off the rails, and you haven't." Their voice rose with a wave to the FBI agents. "We've got someone coming in for the body; can we get a clear path?"

One of the men responded with a petulant pout, but the woman among the three smacked his shoulder and put her hand out for the keys. "Where do you need us?" she asked.

"Just on the street. Thank you. Visible in case we have gawkers or reporters." Mika headed for the sidewalk, dropping their voice for me alone. "I was right."

"About?" I asked.

"You. The analytical chops I expected from your work —" Mika pointed me across to the parking lot of Cherney's work "—and you're solid under pressure."

I frowned as I stepped onto the asphalt, leaving them behind. I'd paused, not firing after the blast.

Yasmine pulled onto the street at the corner and drove toward me. She offered a pleasant smile as she slowed for me and the FBI backing out of the drive. With a tilt of her head, she rolled down her window as I reached the opposite sidewalk. "Mika said headless; how'd we manage that?"

I walked back into the street, not wanting to yell. "The Tarus realm engulfed the upper portion of his body. I'm assuming the draugr got it before coming through." She likely knew enough to make the same deduction.

Her irises were gray with green at the edges to darken them. "How you holding up? The DRC gets into some rough scrapes. This case is pretty active." She seemed genuinely concerned.

"I'm okay." Considering everything we'd been through, I was dealing with it.

She studied me until a pause extended between us, and I broke it, gesturing back toward the parking lot. "Got to grab the car."

"You do that." She pulled forward with a slow squelch of the tires on heating asphalt.

I glanced at the wall of the building where Cherney had escaped down ingenious shields, at the bullet holes left by the other Red Aegis who had ambushed him, then down the side street to the intersection. Had he planned that route, or was he forced to flee there? *An arcanist creating those steps would need time.*

Spent casings littered the parking lot where Olivia had been firing, and a dried stain marked her blood. Police still crowded the entrance to the insurance company, but new officers had replaced those who had been wounded. A single ambulance remained on the street, and EMTs talked to an officer at the back.

The scent of radiator fluid hung in the air. As I strode toward the SUV, several of the police began to pause and watch me. I had no badge, but I recognized at least one face and hoped they'd remember me. No one stopped me as I slid inside the baking heat of the vehicle. Cramped against the wheel, I shifted the seat back.

The damage to the front of the insurance office had taken out the glass of the entrance. One of the police cars had lost a lot of liquid that had drained into the parking lot. A single tech in whites searched the area. *They'll find the clay pieces.* My torn black trash bag lay abandoned against the building. I scrubbed my curls, loosening another piece of confetti. *How does the Consociation lock all this down? Stop the rumors?*

I put the car in reverse, navigating squad cars that had been parked in haste. All were watching as I drove around the back of the insurance agency toward the side street. The FBI had parked just past the entrance where Yasmine had backed in, so I turned right, facing the intersection, and parked under the shade of the Ponderosa pine. The air conditioner churned, but did nothing against the heat. Closer to the intersection with the main street, a taco truck had pulled up to the curb.

As I exited, the team strode toward me, and Dagen veered, pointing. "He cut across the street, heading north. C'mon," she said and took the lead, striding at a quick pace.

Mika kept close to Dagen. Olivia's shoulder was wrapped, and she worked on a pouch while keeping a stride ahead of me.

I found the strongest sense of camaraderie with Olivia. She'd accepted me from the start and hadn't been needling me in the beginning like Mika had.

The three outpaced me, forcing me to quicken my steps.

The main road consisted of five lightly traveled lanes. We jogged to the middle with only one white pickup bearing down on us in the southbound lane. Dagen didn't pause, forcing a dark silver van to honk at us as we ran across the northbound side.

A closed bar lay straight ahead, shaded under Chinese sumacs.

I checked my watch at 10:12 a.m. "It's been half an hour; will you be able to pick up a scent?"

Dagen snorted. "It's Cherney. I've got him." She jogged into the parking lot between the bar and a restaurant, heading for the back where square industrial buildings rose.

I expected her to dead end at one of the parking spaces, but she continued to the back of the restaurant. *Perhaps he's on foot. We couldn't be so lucky.* A large empty lot spread past a stand of sumac, but she turned away toward a fence and alley. In the heat, the dumpster reeked, and I wondered how Dagen could hold her trail with the stench.

The business beside the restaurant narrowed the alley down to the width of a vehicle, while the rough back of some building stood close on the other side of some chain links. The gap between the two corners exposed a plaza beyond the fence that housed an automotive bay. *A long distance to park.* If we'd followed in the SUV, we'd have been stalled.

A guttural scream, long, gurgling, and terrified, sounded from the north. It wasn't close.

Dagen leaped the fence one-handed.

I followed, and we found the first body.

I chased the others across black asphalt as the scream cut short, leaving a silence ahead of us.

At the secluded end of a number of auto repair shops, we jumped the fence at the corner of a stand-alone building with four bays. A dark gray pickup sat in the farthest away, a white sedan perched on a lift in the closest, and the shredded remains of a mechanic lay at the entry to a middle one. I glanced inside the glassed office to my right, where blood stained the windows and the torn corpse of a woman leaned with her back against the door.

"Down here!" Dagen yelled. She ran toward the rear side of the row of auto repair shops. Her boots ground into gravel that filled a less than decorative area with a single elm and some electrical boxes.

Two gunshots echoed from the direction she headed, and I followed with Mika and Olivia beside me. I pulled my weapon, conscious of Dagen's earlier ribbing. *Would I hesitate?*

Cars of all types bordered the edges of the drive, growing thicker farther down. Other vehicles had been parked closer to the back of the building to create a narrow strip barely wide enough to drive through.

Another body lay just twenty feet from our end of the row, sprawled lifeless on the gray concrete. From the damage of the first two corpses, this wasn't Cherney or a gun; we had a cryptid on the loose. So, not Cherney directly, but I had no doubt he'd caused this. He had to be stopped.

There had been no more gunshots, and as Dagen jogged in and out of the edges of the bays, the rest of us caught up.

"Dagen?" Mika called. "What do we have?"

"It's human."

I could see the body ten feet ahead with a face ripped nearly off. Slack skin hung over the lips, peeled back from the ear across the cheek to expose a broken jaw, shattered teeth, and torn flesh. That kind of strength didn't come naturally to any man. As I jogged a step closer, the angle of the neck appeared wrong. *Snapped*.

"Demon?" I asked.

Dagen shrugged, but Olivia nodded in agreement.

"Do you feel anything?" Mika asked with a quick glance at my face.

"What?" I frowned, striding past the ruin of the young mechanic. Beside him lay a discarded open-end wrench, smudged only with grease. Her question made little sense until I considered that we might be facing a demon. They could manipulate human emotions. "No."

My pulse raced, both from the chase and the exertion of the run. I wasn't terrified or enraged. With my left hand, I pulled a detection spell from Haven and slung it down the alley against the building. The cars parked two deep on one side and the dark bays on the other could hide anyone waiting for us.

Dagen, now hazed with a ghost of white, darted out of the next bay, eyes wild. Hairy fuzz had grown on her face, her jaw extended toward a muzzle, and claws hung ready from her fingers. "Another one in the back." She pointed behind her.

The faint hint of Haven lay there, the dead left with a thin afterglow of the detection spell. Two bays down, two more corpses showed as wisps of white. I alerted the others. "What I don't see is anything alive."

About one third of the way to the end, a second building faced the others, and vehicles parked beside bay doors created a narrow alley. I gestured to the last section. "My spell doesn't reach that far."

Dagen took off at a sprint, and I struggled to keep up with them all. The acrid scent of spent gunpowder caught my nose as we passed the bay with two bodies.

I pulled a second detection spell, feeling the strain from using so much magic over the past twenty-four hours with so little sleep. I lobbed it ahead of Dagen, causing a weak pulse of white about her. Another faint body lay in the building to her left, with a brighter hulk roaming in the back. "Left," I shouted to her.

She glanced back, and I pointed. As she sprang behind a parked utility pickup, I pulled a binding.

As the Haven-white behemoth jerked about, Dagen darted toward it.

I felt like a plodding slug as Olivia reached the truck with Mika two strides behind, while I had at least four more paces to reach the bay. In any group of witches, I had no doubt I'd be the fastest, but against a Merfolk, vampire, and werewolf, I came up short.

With a snarl and a low grunt, Dagen and something much larger merged in the white of Haven, then she was tossed away into a clatter of metal. Olivia, slighter than

Dagen, lunged at the bulky figure, coming in low before darting away on her own.

I reached the pickup, peering into the bay as I ran for the back bumper. The pink-faced man's face distorted in rage as he raised a massive crowbar, focusing on Mika two steps in front of him. Dressed in blood-drenched mechanic's overalls, he stood at six and maybe four inches, and couldn't have weighed less than three hundred pounds.

Mika shifted as their gun fired with a spray of fire and smoke, hitting him square in the chest. He still managed a step, crowbar raised. A second shot clouded my view, but he staggered, unsure on his feet. The last bullet opened his forehead just as a black mist began to seep from him. Before the demon fully materialized out of the corpse, it whined an impossibly high shriek, and flashed out of existence.

As I stepped beside Mika, I flinched when metal clattered onto the concrete. The gun smoke hid that the man had dropped his weapon. His body folded at the knees, then slammed forward. The impact vibrated through my sneakers.

"Carl," Olivia said. "He'd been shot in the side. The logo on his uniform is the same as the first man we came across, and the name tag said Carl."

Mika swore and pulled out their cell. "Dagen, Zach, back on Cherney's trail. Olivia and I will deal with the police."

I noted the sirens in the background. They were literally across the street, and they were in no mood to deal with us.

Dagen appeared no worse for her tousle with the demon-infused Carl. "C'mon, gym bro. I lost the scent at the end of this row of buildings. Keep up." As she jogged out of the bay, I holstered my weapon, dismissed my spell, and jumped to follow her.

"Your bullets, they're the special ammo. That demon just vaporized."

"We'll get you some."

My weak spell still showed the ghosts of the people dead in the back of the bay as we passed. Cherney had caused random innocents to die, just to delay us. I could not fathom his thinking; fanatics eluded my understanding. "This might not be the only — diversion," I said.

"What?" Dagen's still-bushy eyebrows dropped, and she glanced around with quick snaps of her head. Her jaw had retracted, mostly, but light fur clung to her cheeks.

"He's got nothing to lose. If the Red Aegis have turned against him, and we're hot on his trail, he might resort to setting off Tarus anywhere he can." I grimaced at the damage he could have done if we weren't close enough to stop Carl.

Dagen swore, then sniffed as we ran back. "He didn't come this way."

Behind the cars parked at the edge of the drive was a fence, then a large open area with semi containers, RVs, and even a boat. Two hundred feet from us, across the storage yard, gray roofs peaked over the tops of the clutter. In the morning heat, no one moved or worked in the place. I scanned, but not even birds moved around us, only the distant hum of traffic and wailing sirens to the north hinted at activity in Reno.

As we passed the dead mechanic in the middle of the drive, my anger rose. Cherney had been willing to let people die in his fanatical attack. He might have set traps for us alone, but he knew the mayhem he'd unleashed, just to cause a delay.

When we were close to the end of the strip of automotive buildings and the lone building where Carl had been possessed, Dagen darted between a rusting Cadillac the size of a boat and a pale blue Pinto. As she took the brush-covered fence in one leap, I shifted to follow with a tight jaw.

She glanced back, as if to confirm she hadn't lost me. "What's gotten to you, gym bro?"

We dashed across a weed-strewn sandy wash toward a container. "He killed all those people."

"Yeah, it gets annoying." Dagen sidestepped a knot of burs growing from a clump of weeds. "Sort of the reason I do this."

I bristled at her cavalier comment. "Killed them."

"People do that."

With an effort, I held my tongue. She wasn't wrong, and I knew the hatred that churned everywhere, but the maliciousness that Cherney exhibited seemed to go beyond the selfish reasons that caused most to resort to violence. *Peter. Beth.* My breath hitched.

Dagen, and the rest of the DRC team, fought deadly problems like this every day. I'd come for vengeance wrapped in a silk bag called justice. After being hurt this morning, she raced into more danger without hesitation, and I accused her of being callous, at least in my thoughts.

Later, I'll ask how she ended up in the DRC.

When we reached the massive container with painted rust, she immediately jogged left down a narrow space between a second wall of metal. My eyes widened, and I tugged on the realms, sure he'd mark a trap for us in such small confines. No wards showed.

We broke through to the far end, and Dagen took us northeast at an angle across a paved drive with gritty yellow sand strewn from a long-gone wind. The trees and low buildings marked the outer edges, with taller buildings rising behind. After six strides, I spotted a heavy, shirtless man standing under the shade of a tree. She ran straight for him, though he peered in the opposite direction. Cherney had nearly an hour on us at this point, so the man couldn't be looking after him.

Above the scuffing of my feet, a faint tinkle of children's voices hovered in the breeze. Two more running paces and their sounds coalesced. A school or daycare from the high pitches. My chest tightened. *They aren't laughing.*

TWENTY

As fast as I'd been running, I found a burst of speed, as if a runner on the last lap.

Dagen too, sprinted faster, and the shirtless man finally heard the sound of our footsteps and turned. He held a beer and stood by a ratty beach chair, peering at us over a wire fence with widening eyes.

When she took the fence with a one-handed spring, he dropped his drink and folded into his chair.

The children were screaming, and at least one adult yelled. The two-story brick building ahead could have been a school. Light green trees and a privacy fence might have secured a playground. My face twitched.

She had three paces on me when we darted beside the house. I tugged at the realms, hoping Cherney hadn't left us a surprise, assuming he'd gone this way. Did Dagen react to the cries or follow a scent?

My phone buzzed in my pocket, but she'd already crossed a small street, aiming for the metal fence threaded with brown plastic strips for privacy. I cursed being slower than her as she disappeared over the top, dropping into the bright green branches.

At six feet, I couldn't pirouette over as she had, but caught the top and kicked my toes into rattling links. From the top, I spotted her crouching on the other side of a thick trunk. Her hand lay on her weapon, but she hadn't drawn it. Children in vibrant colors clustered at the back of the building and pressed to get through the double doors. A worried woman looked out into the yard while her hands hovered over the children as if willing them to hurry and escape.

I landed on the grass with a clear sight of the revenant.

Black and gaseous, a shadow in bright light, it floated at the back of the playground in a near-human form. It ignored the children, us, and the gym with slides, cruising across a colorfully painted four-square and a thin fence beyond. The cryptid would search for the dead, craving to reanimate them and return to a twisted form of life.

With a quick pull into Dur-Alf, I drew a binding spell and sent it flying the eighty feet between us.

The revenant must have gotten a sense of death as it turned and floated through the low fence between the playground and the school's parking lot. My spell flew uselessly past while the cryptid struggled through the metal links.

"It'll take one of our rounds to kill it." Dagen snatched a glance at the retreating children and teachers. "You catch it, then hide me from sight while I shoot it. We can't do anything about the noise."

"Okay." I had no real knowledge of these cryptids beyond the rare report.

I readied another binding while we both stalked after the revenant, who now eased at an increasing speed between cars toward a ragged fence in the back of the lot. On the other side, trailers lay in no particular order across a storage area behind a gray metal building. Trees shaded the rear of the property, and the cryptid floated in their direction.

A man barked from near the school. "What are you doing?" Armed with a walkie-talkie, he wore a guard's uniform.

"FBI," called Dagen, without turning from her prey. In a lower voice, she cursed. "Jackass. Like *we're* your problem." I could have sworn that an accent, perhaps English, flavored her words.

We jumped the fence as the cryptid reached the next. The front of a pickup blocked me from a clear shot with my binding, so I held it. The shadowed entity blended with the shade of the trees as it struggled through more chain link.

"There's something dead back there." Dagen wrinkled her widened nose, distorted with the faint fur.

Visions of any number of zombie movies flashed in my head, and I considered pulling my weapon, for as little good as it would do.

We reached the tall fence at the back, slatted with privacy strips, though many had been broken, leaving sections missing. I pulled my hand from where it wavered by my holster, plucked into Haven, and lit us and the revenant in faint white.

Dagen sprang, taking the fence in one leap with a roll at the top. I scurried behind her, rattling in the quiet. The sounds of children and security guards were long gone, hidden in the school. Even the sirens had faded, likely reaching the last scene of death that Cherney had left.

If his last portal had let through a draugr, demon, or ghoul, the schoolyard would have been a massacre. My jaw ached.

Tagged with my ghostly detection spell, the revenant

flew quickly along the shade of the trees about ten yards ahead of us. Dagen jogged forward, slowly enough that I could keep at her side.

We were twenty feet away when the revenant coalesced into a small spot on the ground. Dagen drew her weapon. "Get ready." She couldn't see the dark-green glowing spell I held in my fingers.

To keep the tree trunks clear from my sight, I moved to the left as we hunted. It meant hopping over the hitch of a beat-up trailer, but I'd have a better shot.

As I threw, the possessed corpse of a rabbit jumped erratically across the sand and weeds. Over a foot long, it lacked a stomach and most of one back leg. The pale fur had darkened to gray, and it regarded us with empty eye sockets. My spell sank into the ground behind it.

Its next hop appeared more coordinated, adjusting to the missing bones of the back foot.

Dagen cursed. "Bind it." She glanced about with her weapon in hand.

With a quick pull and throw, I sent the binding spell the short distance, hitting the revenant-possessed rabbit.

"Hide us." Dagen nodded to the side where a man stood in the parking lot.

We'd just been in a gunfight in the middle of a road, but I didn't argue. I pulled from Mer and wrapped a muddy illusion of me, her, and the rotting rabbit from prying eyes. "Done."

She shot the rabbit, which I could clearly smell. Its head splattered open.

The revenant sprang from it, unfolding into darkness as tall as me. When she put a second bullet through it, a hole appeared and grew until the mist vaporized.

Dagen grumbled curses, holstered her gun, and rolled

her eyes. "Send Mika these coordinates. Update her. I'll deal with this jerk."

The man had his phone out, taking pictures of the two crazies in the storage area killing a dead rabbit — trying, at least. I dismissed my illusion and retrieved my cell.

With a saunter, Dagen waved her badge. "All clear. We've got a case of rabies we're trying to control. Stay out of this area for a while until we get someone out."

I pulled up the coordinates on the map and sent a text to Mika, who had been the one calling me earlier.

REVENANT INCORPORATED A RABBIT AT THIS LOCATION. DISPATCHED.

WE'LL SEND A CLEANUP. WE'RE AT AUTO SHOP. WHAT HAPPENED?

DEMON. DISPATCHED. I guessed she just needed to know there wasn't something lurking there.

OKAY. WE'LL DEAL WITH LOCALS. CHERNEY?

Dagen laughed at something the man said, but I could hear the tightness in her voice.

WE'LL GET BACK TO IT. I assumed. Any guilt I'd had for wanting Cherney dead was long gone.

When we scrambled back over fences to the location where she'd last had his scent, Dagen did so less acrobatically. I could feel the entire neighborhood watching us.

She hit the side road, and we picked up our pace to a quick jog, heading north until we reached the main street. There, she turned at the corner of a bright green pub, walked back and forth along the empty parking spaces out front, then swore. "He was parked here." She spun slowly, studying the buildings around. "See any cameras?"

I didn't. The closest were at the school, and they wouldn't catch this spot.

She pulled out her phone, motioning for us to walk west. "Mika, he's got a ride or car. Off my radar."

My T-shirt stuck to my skin under the vest, and I thought of my water bottle in the SUV. The temperature climbed toward eighty as we walked.

"Yeah. I had to put a couple of rounds into a dead rabbit and a revenant. They'll need to be collected. You at the auto repair strip?"

A squad car raced up the street on the other side of the school, chirping its sirens. I stared at the road and traffic, my eyes glazing.

"On our way."

Cherney had a vehicle, or a driver. His moves had been clever and calculated, lacking any concern for others. *And we have no idea where he is.*

"Need to polish your spell work. Phistrel would want a better replacement."

It took me a long second to realize that Dagen had hung up and addressed me. "Yeah. Not much use for it in analytics." I frowned. "Replacement?"

"Mika wants you on the team, and despite my best judgment, I'm beginning to agree."

I wiped off my brow. "Don't I get a say?"

"Have you met Mika?" She chuckled. "Persuasive is a mild term. Besides, you're good at the thinking part." With a stiff finger, she tapped on my temple, exposing Ya-Keya.

Ahead of us, an ambulance pulled into a drive. It hadn't bothered with lights or siren. *Because they're all dead.* Maybe I *would* join the DRC once we dealt with Cherney.

"I was working security for the Consociation in New York," Dagen said, waiting for me to respond.

"When?"

She smiled. "In '96. We'd had a nasty incursion by one of Iliodor's factions, and I'd done a fair job of cleaning it up. Yasmine wanted to move into forensics. The Consociation wanted to 'diversify' by allowing werewolves and vampires into positions. Mika isn't as prejudiced as some Merfolk. She recruited me."

"Did you want the job?" We were close to the drive that led into the auto repair shops; I recognized the buildings.

"I'd only been in the US for seven years, didn't have much of a social life, so, yeah, I was up for something new, just not the DRC."

"Why not?"

"Didn't want someone bossing me around every minute. Security was bad enough, but I had a set routine and not much hassle."

Flashing lights flooded the buildings down the drive where the demon-possessed Carl had gone on his killing rampage. Dagen opened her mouth to continue, then answered her phone. "We're almost there."

Her face darkened. "We're on the main road, east of the exit. We'll wait." She hung up.

"What?" I asked.

"Neddie's tracking all emergency calls, since the police are less than cooperative at the moment, and picked up a report of a paralyzed man in an industrial area." Dagen stood on the sidewalk, peering down the street expectantly.

"She thinks it's a binding spell." I nodded. "Which could either be Cherney or the shooter who escaped."

TWENTY-ONE

As we stood at the side of the road waiting for Mika and breathing exhaust, I glanced back at the pub where Cherney had parked. How had he known to ambush us at the insurance agency?

He'd found a vehicle; Neddie would have spotted his credit transaction if he'd rented one, stowed it a quarter-mile away, and planned his escape. It was too much of a coincidence that he'd done all this without knowing if we'd be back at his office.

"What are you staring at?" Dagen asked, breaking my thoughts.

I shook my glazed eyes off the white sedan parked to our left. "Nothing. Just thinking."

"And?" Her fingers dug through her orange hair that had stiffened with moisture.

"This is all a bit of a coincidence, don't you think?"

She gestured to the team's SUV driving toward us. "Figured he followed us somehow." Her slight frown hinted that she had just now considered the situation.

That *was* possible. Olivia and I had spent a good bit of

time cleaning up. Cherney could have followed us, then retreated to the pub, and headed back on foot. *He would have risked missing us.*

Dagen popped open the rear door and gestured for me to slide across to sit behind the driver's seat.

Mika handed me a charging case with two comms earbuds. "We've identified the victim as Charlie Miles. Driver for a local gas company. His truck is missing."

Dagen slammed her door and groaned as she took a set of comms. "I hate these things."

"We might get separated again." Mika pulled back a strand of pink hair, studying me. "What do you think they'll do with the truck?"

"Blow something up," Dagen snorted.

I nodded in agreement. *But, why?* "Could they be baiting us?"

With a gesture, Mika urged me to continue.

"Leaving the binding on the driver instead of just killing him, so that we'd be alerted, seems like an intentional move. Now, we have a gas truck to rescue before more innocent people are hurt, so we'll head there. A trap." I pulled up my water bottle, suddenly parched.

"A reasonable possibility," Mika agreed.

After no one else jumped in, I continued. "We just got ambushed while investigating a threat at the insurance office. An employee gets injured digging in Cherney's files, we arrive to clear the area, and Cherney drops curse tokens on us. He went through a lot of effort to attack us, so it stands to reason he planned it. There are patterns here."

Olivia spoke, "An operating procedure out of a playbook."

Dagen huffed. "The Red Aegis playbook."

Mika's head bobbed. "How can we use it?"

"Be careful," said Dagen.

I stared out the front windshield. Traffic had grown heavy. *Why had the employee gone digging in Cherney's warded box?* "What if Cherney contacted his coworker at the office and sent him to set off the ward on some pretext? Purely to get us out there."

With a nod, Mika pulled out their phone, facing front. "Neddie. Can you check if an agent at the insurance agency named Stroupe received any messages or calls between the time we left until he was sent to the hospital?"

A second passed, and Mika answered. "Good idea. Yes."

After a moment, Neddie spoke over the speaker. "I've got a flag on the spam comments that Cherney deleted. There's a repetitious set with only a couple of words altered in each. Some type of code. I've sent it down south for a colleague to look at. I'll let you know if we break it. I'll pull up the personal phone records for Stroupe and those of the agency. Won't take a minute." Her serious tone shifted with a light cackle. "We're so damned busy that I've got Isaac working for me."

"Thanks, Neddie. Let us know." Mika hung up, then twisted about to face me. "Good call on the spam."

Olivia stopped with a line of cars at an intersection and glanced at Mika. "Neddie will have the site flagged, so if they use it to communicate again, we'll know. It will be more helpful if we can decode it."

We'd been one step behind Cherney and the Red Aegis and in the dark about what conflict went on between them, but I was more concerned about the first. If we could get an idea of what they planned next, then we might gain an advantage. *We're all bait*, I thought, *just like we'd planned to use me.*

As I finished my water, I pulled up Neddie's reports,

searching for the newest on the missing gas truck. It had been taken after exiting a gas company in an industrial area. A blasting ward might pierce the tank and certainly a valve. The explosion, though not fiery itself, might cause torn metal to spark. *Where?* The target's whereabouts might get us ahead of whoever planned the trap.

I opened a map and scrolled through the area. No school or mall was close. The gas company had some major tanks. Perhaps they intended to blow that up and ambush us when we arrived.

"Where are we headed?" I asked.

Mika turned. "To the site where the driver was found."

"Can we check the business he worked for first?"

"Of course. Why?"

"If the truck is a bomb, then setting off the entire property might bring us to the location. Unless just hijacking the truck is enough. We might get word that it's been spotted outside a school or mall. Anonymous tip. Until then, I'd look for the truck back at the company, warded to explode when they find it."

"They may very well plan on our looking there," offered Olivia.

My lips pursed. "You might be right."

I zoomed in and out on the map of the location. "There's a complex east of the gas company that has high visibility. In every other direction, they'd have to get too close and put themselves at risk. The river to the south blocks all but a bicycle trail."

"That might offer a good escape," said Olivia. "How far from a potential explosion?"

"A couple hundred feet." I gauged the distance from the larger tanks, but the company had storage all over the property. "What could Cherney or one of them do from a range greater than that?"

We turned at an intersection, and I capped my empty water bottle, waiting for a response.

Olivia spoke. "I believe we have optional outcomes. One, they have a rifle with longer accuracy. Two, we have misinterpreted the target and location. Three, they are willing to risk a closer engagement with no expectation of an explosion."

"Four, they're suicidal fanatics that plan to leave us all in a crater." Dagen huffed. "We ain't going to think our way out of this one."

Olivia turned us off the main road into an industrial district, and I considered Dagen's comment. The Red Aegis had been careful zealots, reactivating their vision with Cherney's downloads of rituals that opened Tarus. *They're not suicide bombers.*

Mika ran a hand through their hair. "Let me and Dagen out just short of the gas company. Give us five minutes. Olivia, cover Zach while he searches for wards, the truck, or anything that reeks of the Red Aegis. Comms on."

I tapped on the earbuds, and an ambient hum started. After the deafening blast, I still had an occasional ringing despite Everek's healing.

"Testing," Dagen said, but the comms were too close and resisted transmission.

Neddie's voice surprised me. "Shit must be serious if you've got comms on Dagen. Everybody on?"

"Yes," said Mika.

"Good. I'll still send a report, but sharp shot on looking for a call to Stroupe. Ten minutes before he lost his left hand, he got a call from a prepaid. Don't get excited; it's turned off at present. However, it did help in another area since I checked its call logs. I've got two other burners connected to it, both off, but we're tracking, and, most importantly, an FBI officer who works in cybersecurity could have tipped off Cherney about Zach's request."

My jaw tightened, and the skin on my cheeks crawled. *The mole.*

"Isaac has sent orders to pick him up. I'll keep you informed. Also, sent you a report on the man who lost his head; glad you got me a *before* photograph. High confidence on Lex Unger, a fifty-two-year-old tech support out of Bakersfield, California. Light arcane rating. I'm tracking his communications and analyzing social media. Go me. Happy hunting."

Olivia pulled to a stop with two low industrial buildings close on each side. Mika pulled the blue of Mer and became invisible.

Dagen hopped out, eager, and closed her door. "Where do you want me, boss?" came clearly over the comms.

"Other side of the building to the south is a large parking lot. Give it a lap, then head to the bike trail by the river. I'll head to the other lot to the east. We'll have Olivia and Zach between us."

Dagen took off down the road behind us. "Still think it's a wild goose chase, gym bro?"

I remained in the back, while Olivia idled in place. The gas company would be the next entrance on our right, two hundred feet ahead. "Water?" I asked Olivia as I reached into the back.

"No, thank you."

While I sipped lukewarm water, I stared out the front windshield. Blanchard had stumbled upon a conversation with Cherney that held some importance. *What did stampede mean?* Perhaps a code name for a project?

"Neddie," I asked over the comms, "can I ask you a question? Have you researched 'stampede' around Reno?"

"Yeah, some rodeos mention it in marketing, but no

locale or event in Reno. There's a slot machine named stampede. Calgary is nicknamed Stampede City. A reservoir in California about thirty miles away."

I sat in silence for a minute before I responded. "Is there a town near the reservoir?"

"Give me a sec."

What task am I taking her away from? She hadn't continued the brusque reaction to me since we met in Phoenix.

"There's jack shit around the reservoir until you get about fifteen miles south of it. Town called Truckee. I've got a campground near the water; that's it."

Olivia started to move forward.

"Any chance we could see if someone booked a site this weekend but hasn't arrived yet?"

She sniffed. "What's one more thing?" Her tone wasn't insulted or angry, just frustrated, as we all were.

"Thanks." I studied the street ahead, the gate, and the quiet building at the corner. As we pulled up to the gate, Olivia parked.

"That matches the description of the gas truck," she said, turning off the engine and pointing out the passenger window.

It wasn't huge, for a gas truck, but the silos next to it were. *Crap*.

TWENTY-TWO

When I stepped out of the car, I tossed a detection spell into the dirt parking area to our left. Olivia glowed, but the brush and barricades remained dark.

"I don't see anyone in the vicinity." She scanned with quick, jerky movements.

Petroleum and sulfur wafted in the air while dull clanging, like that of someone working on equipment, rang from far ahead where I assumed Mika scouted. With careful footsteps, we stalked toward the gate while I tugged at the realms.

"No apparent wards." My voice low, it scraped out in a dry rasp.

I sent a second Haven spell to the fuel tanks, dusty white silos at least two stories high. A figure in the building near the SUV ghosted inside the walls, appearing to be seated at a desk. Razor wire looped along the top of the fence and the open gate. Cars and trucks parked in the lot, including one massive tanker and our smaller tank truck. Containers and a large shed blocked the back. The buildings I could see beyond the low structures of the yard would be optimal, if our ambusher planned to use a rifle.

Olivia craned her neck to gain a view of the rear of the business. More tank trucks parked there, but everyone appeared happy to stay inside as the sun hung high overhead, approaching noon. "Do you think this is unusually quiet?" she asked.

My energy sagging, I pulled another detection spell and sent it to the back of the gas company's building. Half a dozen faint white figures were sitting, standing, or walking in what seemed normal activity. "There's six people inside, and they seem to be working." I gestured to the gas truck, about sixty feet ahead. "Let me take this last bit on my own. There's nobody near it."

She stopped, eyes flitting. Her demeanor reminded me of a bird — not a nervous wren, but a predator, alert at every possibility.

After ten careful paces, I tugged at the realms, quickly spotting three Dur-Alf blasting wards on the vehicle. The most obvious overlapped the door and handle, so that any attempt to move it would set it off. The other two were nearby on the tank itself. "It's warded," I said over the comms. "I'm going to disarm them."

My sneakers ground sand and pebbles against the asphalt, and sweat trickled down my temples. The temperature had topped eighty under the merciless sun.

I tugged at the threads of Dur-Alf from four paces away, unraveling the first ward over the door. Constructed of oil, the sigil shone in the sun, except one section at the bottom. With the thickness of a pencil lead, a white substance sagged, threatening to break the ward. *Wax?*

With quick but careful tugs, I worked on the next wards. "They're using wax for parts of the sigils," I said in a muted tone, as if I might disturb the traps. "It's a timer, of sorts, with the sun as hot as it is." The realms connected to the medium used for the sigils, and triggering the ward only took breaking that substance. As I disarmed the last, my back prickled, waiting for some sniper's shot.

"Don't open the truck. I'm heading over," Mika said over the comms. "The area to the east is clear. Everyone is inside. Dagen?"

"Baking over on the bicycle trail. Where do you need me, boss?"

"Can you see Zach from there?"

"I'd have to go up to the fence."

"Do that. Then stay put."

"From Zach's observation, I believe we are early," said Olivia.

I agreed, but remained silent. The wax dripped away, breaking the now-defunct ward. *Early by sixty seconds.*

Olivia stood watching, turning at times to view the road where our SUV waited. I felt exposed. How would whoever placed this react when their explosion didn't happen? Would they retreat, or move in?

The clanging to the east stopped, leaving only a distant highway humming in the midday silence. It felt eerie, like the pause in a horror movie.

A scuff sounded behind me and I started, whirling about. While Olivia studied me with wide eyes, Mika chuckled as they both approached.

"Just us." With a pull into Mer, Mika wrapped Olivia in invisibility, enveloping her in blue. When they reached the truck, Mika used a lifting spell to float our comrade over the windshield. "Anything?"

"Nothing I can see."

I frowned, causing Olivia to continue. "I'm looking to see if there are any mechanical detonators. The Red Aegis repository of information urges its acolyte arcanists to blend technology with the arcane. In regard to traps, we found this true in Montana."

Need to read that report all the way through. I scanned the surrounding area, waiting for the ambush.

Mika nudged their chin toward me. "What do you think? Red herring? Maybe someone wanted us diverted, or was their whole plan to blow up this oil company?"

Over the fence, the silos rose well-protected, but I still stepped over and tugged at the realms to search for wards. Nothing. What was the point of all this?

"What I think," said Dagen, "is that someone is taking a piss. They just want us out here running about."

Somewhere to the east of us, a car alarm blared. Mika brought Olivia back in a quick snap, then removed the illusion. "Dagen, move east on that bike trail. Olivia, grab the car. Zach, keep up with me."

I'd barely reached the road before Mika outpaced me by ten strides. The alarm beeped rhythmically on the far side of the public works building, a long structure with closed bay doors. Under the vest, sweat soaked my T-shirt.

Olivia fired up the SUV behind me.

Ahead, a cluster of men exited a door, glancing about at the noise, noticing us, but still wandering toward their cars. Lunchtime.

"Boss, we got a problem." From Dagen's voice, I gathered she was running. "I've got something running on the other side of the river. Ghoul. Draugr. Something without bike shorts. There's a bridge I'm heading to now."

Mika flicked a glance over their shoulder at me and Olivia. "Zach, Olivia, see what's going on with that car. It might be nothing."

I'd run a good two hundred yards when Mika disappeared behind the maintenance building. The alarm blared from the parking lot full of vehicles. A man and a woman had stopped at a red sedan to watch Mika race south.

Olivia passed me, accelerating. As she turned right into the parking lot, the asphalt exploded under her front tire with a flash of Dur-Alf. After the initial bounce, the SUV ground to a stop with the axle buckling under the hood.

Mika called over the comms, "Olivia?"

A moment ticked away as I closed the distance.

"I'm okay." Olivia's voice did not have its usual focused tone; she sounded dazed. "Go."

As I neared the gaping hole in the asphalt, four feet wide and half that deep, I tugged at Dur-Alf. Curse coins littered the area. Mika had missed them, cutting between bright yellow bumpers surrounding a light pole.

"Curse coins," I called over the comms.

Acrid gasoline hung in the air as I darted around the clay tokens. None lay close to where the SUV had come to a grinding halt.

A man swore in the parking lot where the alarm had led us. There were more people exiting the maintenance building and heading out for lunch.

Olivia pried open her mangled driver's door with a squeal of metal. She didn't turn to me, but focused on the cars ahead.

Blood covered the windshield of a white pickup where a ghoul smashed at the crumbling glass, breaking free. The occupant of the truck had likely set off a ward that opened Tarus. The couple moved in a panicked hurry to get inside their sedan, only two rows away. As the lunchtime crowd spotted the cryptid, they retreated for the building's doors.

I locked onto the cryptid, but Olivia already had a lead on me.

Dagen swore. "My friend just smashed through a window to get some rubbernecking idiots. Mika, two-story brick this side of the river. Some sort of glass front. Heading inside."

The ghoul, its torso covered in blood, crouched on the hood to survey the lot. My anger at the cryptid came more from my experience with losing Peter and Beth than it did with the danger it presented.

Olivia's cooler, analytical tone had returned when she spoke. "Ghoul. One dead already."

"I'm sending Everek and Yasmine to your location," said Neddie.

Whoever had drawn us here hadn't attempted an ambush yet, but they were willing to let plenty of people die in the meantime. I could only hope they intended to show up to the mayhem that they'd created. I drew my weapon and plucked a binding spell.

TWENTY-THREE

With my gun hand, I brushed on the realms in case our antagonist had left more traps. Metal shrieked in the lot as the man driving the sedan drove into the side of another car. I hadn't had time to clear the curse coins, but couldn't take my focus off the ghoul.

The cryptid had seen Olivia, and perhaps sated from its meal or recognizing her nature, it opted to leap off the pickup and dart between the row of parked cars. At least as fast as her, it disappeared from my sight.

"In pursuit," she said over the comms, "heading south."

In response, glass shattered near Dagen or Mika.

I dashed to keep up with Olivia and our ghoul, with my gun in one hand and a binding spell in the other. Thirty yards ahead of me, the cryptid raced into the open after the last cluster of cars. A line of trees rose two hundred feet at the rear, likely where the river lay.

In the rows of parked cars, I passed a woman crouched in the shade of a utility truck so low that her hands pressed on the asphalt. Her brown hair spilled onto the ground, and her wide eyes tracked my strides.

"Get inside." With my gun, I pointed toward the building where she might have some modicum of safety. Any of the cars could be trapped. My scan flicked about the lot, searching for the architect of the ambush. *Where is he?*

Muffled screams echoed over the comms, and Dagen swore. "Little shithead's running upstairs. Mika?"

"Almost to the building." Mika's voice sounded calm with only a hint of exertion, while I'd resorted to breathing through my mouth.

In my groups of coworkers, musicians, and friends, I'd been considered the healthy, athletic one, while against a vampire, Merfolk, and werewolf I felt like a couch potato out for their first jog.

Our ghoul hit the fence at the back of the lot, trying to crash through as if it were mere brambles in a forest. Olivia had twenty yards before she'd catch up to it, and she might before it figured out how to climb over.

A scream sounded behind me, and I spun to a stop.

The woman had not taken my advice, and a draugr climbed through a dark cloud of Tarus pouring out of a pale silver compact. Too distant for me to risk a shot, she backed away from the cryptid between the closely parked vehicles.

"I've got a draugr. Olivia?" After a day with them, I had no doubt she could handle herself.

"Go," she called back over the comms.

I sprinted, but the woman never had a chance. Her shriek ended as the draugr shredded her head and neck, spraying the cars nearby with dark red. My teeth ground in a resurgence of anger and frustration over our hidden ambusher.

Closer to the building, a second scream sounded from a man who'd exited to witness the brutal slaying. The fool lucked out, as the draugr only had eyes for me.

The cryptid leaped onto the hood of a car, adjusting as the metal sagged under its weight. With a quick spring, it reached the roof of a pickup, then gained speed as it moved to the next vehicle.

Bring it.

I'd covered thirty feet and stopped when I had its attention. The shot I fired would have little effect without specialized ammunition, but I used it for two purposes: first, to warn anyone else who intended to run for their cars, and second, to slow the cryptid, if even for a moment.

The latter worked as I clipped the draugr in the upper chest, forcing it to stumble and regain its footing on a white Prius. However, my binding slipped off its right side, failing to wrap around the gray bulk.

As it leaped for a yellow sedan at the end of the row, I stunned it with a second shot and sent another binding a moment after. The bullet hit, but the spell slipped off with only nine yards of open asphalt between me and the draugr. The pink tones in the depths of its skinless muscles were visible, and my pulse spiked.

Dagen swore as glass crashed over the comms.

When its feet hit the ground, I felt, or at least imagined, the weight of it vibrate through my sneakers. My mind had never had the opportunity for fear when I'd crushed the ghoul who had slaughtered Beth and Peter, but now I drew a shaky inhale through my nose. *I should have asked Mika about ammo.*

As it launched toward me, each stride eating over a yard, I brushed my gun hand against Dur-Alf to form a shield to my right and readied a binding spell in my left. If I missed, I'd prepared a slim chance to survive.

When its right foot landed, the skinless toes slapped with a disturbing wet noise akin to a fish hitting a dock. The two bullets I'd put into it were angry red puckers in its upper chest. Stretched white-gray, the draugr's lips pulled tight to expose stained teeth.

My held breath tightened in my chest as I waited for one last stride. *Can't miss. Don't miss.*

One of the four-foot-long arms pulled back, ready to strike at my unprotected left side. The heavy footfall vibrated the asphalt, and I lobbed my spell underhand, like a weak softball pitch. Speed mattered less than accuracy.

The draugr noticed the movement, raking at my outstretched hand with its other arm.

Its thick black claws scraped without a sound into my shield while my binding spell struck where a bellybutton should have been. The mossy-green filaments wound around the creature's side.

I fell, more than stepped, back in retreat, keeping the shield between us with a slight shift to the side.

The spell connected behind the draugr's stomach, and I felt it lock into place. The sensation was always satisfying, but in this case it released my breath in a huff of a laugh.

The draugr stiffened, with one arm raised to strike, the other stunted against my shield, and a leg poised in the air, mid-stride. Its momentum carried it into my shield, then spun the cryptid to the ground, dark eyes locked on mine.

Peter and Beth once again flashed in my memory as I pulled a crushing spell from Dur-Alf and slammed it down with cold ferocity rather than rage. Unlike the ghoul, little liquid oozed out, but the shattered bones pierced the gray muscle and cut black lines through it.

"Olivia?" My voice, a mere whisper, croaked from my lips.

"I've got it cornered at the water. I can help in a minute."

"I'm clear." I scanned south, where Olivia, Mika, and Dagen had gone. "I'll come to you." My head turned to the rows of parked cars, then to the distant doors of the building where people likely watched, or waited to race to their deaths if there were more wards set. "Actually, I should clear these cars of wards, if that's okay."

"We're good," said Mika, though their breath sounded rough, as if running.

With the second attempt, I holstered my gun, turned to walk between the bumpers of the cars, and tugged at the realms. In a few seconds, I reached the slaughtered woman, a tangle of flesh, hair, and blood. Sweat had run under my vest, soaking my pants.

Water splashed, and Olivia grunted. "Ghoul down, sending Neddie the coordinates for removal. Mika?"

"We're fine," Dagen answered over the comms. "Little puck's a runner."

"Get back to Zach, we've almost got it," Mika responded.

Near the woman's car, I located another Tarus sigil on the driver's headrest of a black BMW. With the door unlocked, I opened it carefully and unraveled the ward. As I moved to the next block of vehicles, I could see the pickup where the first ghoul had broken through the wind-shield. The playbook used by the Red Aegis seemed partic-ularly nasty. First, I imagined the occupant sliding into the seat, closing the door, then leaning their head back; a portal to Tarus would have filled the cab. *Like in the tent.*

Beside the truck was another warded sedan. I had only one more block of cars to check on this row. The cars farther out were alone and spread out.

The ruined SUV we'd been driving tilted into the

ground like a wounded animal. Beyond it, three people stood by their cars in a far parking lot, watching me. Another waited in the shaded doorway of a low beige building. They would have witnessed all of it.

Dagen swore with a triumphant tone.

While I glanced back to the south, noting Olivia climbing a fence by the river, an engine sounded from where the onlookers lingered. A white work truck pulled from the lot, driven by a pale man with a brimmed hat and sunglasses. I continued my search, but kept a wary eye on the spectator.

As he turned to exit the parking area, directly in line with the team's SUV, a gun flash lit at the edge of his rolled-down window.

The windshield between me and him shattered into a spiderweb of glass with a single dark hole. A second shot ricocheted off the roof, and a third clanged into something metallic, but by that time, I'd crouched down to the bumpers to draw my weapon. I scrambled backward and alongside the car.

"Zach? Olivia?"

The vehicle tore down the road we'd arrived on, disappearing behind the corner of the building as I reached the back of the car, still moving low for cover.

"White work truck. Novelty Nevada license containing 358 with a fourth number of 8 or 9. Driver's white. Not Cherney, unless he's shaved. Wearing sunglasses and hat. Gray shirt. I'd guess a 9mm."

Sirens called from a distant street. With a slow rise, I clocked the three onlookers jogging toward the building. *Good call.*

I should probably check those cars as well.

"For an ambush, this seems sloppy," I stated to none of them in particular.

"It could have been worse," Mika said. "If the gas company had gone up, we'd have had almost half a dozen cryptids on our hands, dividing our attention and possibly overwhelming one of us."

Dagen huffed, indignant.

Maybe we had gotten here in time. We had disarmed two of the wards.

"We've still got two of the Red Aegis on the loose," I said, trying to keep the discouragement out of my voice.

Neddie spoke over the comms in a cheerful tone. "Might have some joy on that. Cherney's burner just went live."

CHAPTER
TWENTY-FOUR

I turned to the south, where Olivia jogged across the parking lot. Mika and Dagen had been on the opposite side of the river. Instead of hogging the comms with useless questions, I waited.

"Do we have FBI on their way?" Mika asked. "Our vehicle's down."

"Police will be here soon enough." Dagen snorted. "Don't suppose they'll let us borrow a vehicle."

"Shush, child," Neddie said over the comms. "I'll push. They're raising a ruckus about manpower. Everek and Yasmine were just finishing up at the insurance agency, so I'll see if the FBI there can be dispatched to your location. I'll break the news of you commandeering their vehicle when they get to you."

"They can have ours. Just let me grab my bag." Dagen's lighthearted attempt went ignored.

Their speech paced with running, Mika spoke. "Do what you can, Neddie. Thanks."

I waited, then informed Mika of the wards I'd found,

only to be told, "Clear as much of the lot as possible. We'll be there in two minutes."

The stifling air carried the scent of hot asphalt and baking cars. Sirens sounded from the west, and the murmur of highway traffic rumbled to the east.

Olivia reached me as I darted between the cars of the back row. "How many wards?" she asked.

With a quick gesture along the row closer to the building, I answered, "Four, if you count the two that were triggered."

She kept up. "How long would that take?"

The traps had been in pairs of vehicles side-by-side, so I considered for a moment. "Including breaking into the cars, maybe fifteen to twenty minutes." She was building a timeline.

"Where was he parked, before he shot at you?"

I motioned to the far lot. "There. Think we should check there?"

"Do you?" she asked.

As we reached the last vehicle except for a farther line of maintenance trucks, some with plows, I shook my head. "Too little time; he wouldn't want to have a cryptid to deal with when the employees came out for their cars at lunchtime."

"I concur." She turned from me to focus on Mika and Dagen sprinting from the fence and the river.

A squad car had pulled to the front of the maintenance building, just out of our sight, but its lights lit the vehicles there. More sirens called from the direction of the road. "What do you tell them?" I asked Olivia. "The local police. It's rarely in the files except for 'reported as an animal attack' or some such."

"Pretty much that," said Mika over the comms. The two of them were halfway across the lot, heading for the draugr that I'd mashed. "We need to clear the ammo out. If you're done, meet us there." They drew the blue of Mer, washing the cryptid with an illusion.

Under the brutal midday sun, I reluctantly began to jog behind Olivia, my clothes sticking to me. I didn't know the biological needs of vampires, Merfolk, or werewolves, but I needed water in eighty-degree heat. Running and exercising in Phoenix kept me aware of the importance.

We met the others at the rear of the ruined SUV as Dagen opened the back hatch. Of the four of us, only Olivia wasn't sweating. I began disarming the curse coins scattered on the road.

Mika's pink hair had darkened, matted to their head. "Neddie? Update on FBI. Cherney's phone still on?"

"I've got some arrogant Special Agent in Charge Aston headed your way. Bet he'll be fun to separate from his vehicle. Cherney's hunkered down. No calls or incoming data. I'd be suspicious. I've updated Lily. She's disappointed about our boy losing his head, but plans on being available when you can keep one alive."

Dagen waved me over and handed me a heavy ammo case.

Olivia turned. "Mika."

From the front entrance of the maintenance facility, a hefty officer spotted our activity and jogged toward us. At the doorway, another officer spoke with a pair of timid employees who peered about, expecting another cryptid based on their wide eyes.

Mika waved a badge toward the policeman. "Keep everyone inside."

Two more squad cars tore down the road near the gas company, lights flashing. The man, sporting a light-brown graying mustache and heavy jowls, didn't appear interested in the credentials.

"We need to evacuate everyone. Now." He scuffed to a stop just two feet from Mika, obviously attempting to intimidate. "Whatever bullshit is going on — I've got people losing it, reporting — whatever."

"Fair," said Mika with a flourish toward the crater in the asphalt. "We've tracked down at least two terrorists who've set mines and booby-trapped vehicles. Everyone leaves on foot until the FBI clears the area."

His eyes scanned the hole, our damaged vehicle, and finally the parking lot while his lips worked in silence and his cheeks puffed.

Mika nodded to the squad cars barreling toward us, and the man pinched his radio to yell out a warning as he waved them down with his free hand.

We continued to empty out the SUV, placing three bags, the ammo case, and a cooler of water onto the asphalt. I helped myself to one while heading to the passenger door to retrieve my bottle. It had a NIN sticker on it that I'd grown fond of. After I retrieved it, I stared off at the beige building where a pair of the employees had grown curious enough to step out and watch the police.

"Why is Cherney leaving his phone on?" I asked.

"A trap?" asked Olivia. "How far away, Neddie?"

A sigh came over the comms, then distinct typing. "Ten to twelve minutes at this time of day. Lunch traffic."

Olivia watched me. "If that's Cherney's phone, then he wasn't the one who shot at you."

"Agreed," I said. "They're both Red Aegis, and both want us dead, but they're also after each other."

"Does their mutual animosity make sense, given what you know of them?" she asked.

"Too little information." I finished the water, tossed the bottle into the emptied back of the SUV, and grabbed another.

"We could hope that Cherney's dead," offered Dagen.

My reaction surprised me. At this point, I didn't need to understand his intentions when he loosed the draugr on my family, so whether or not he died at our hands, I no longer cared. He could offer me no satisfactory answer to taking Beth and Peter from me. However, I would feel cheated if someone else did it. "That's a possibility. Perhaps the two know each other well enough that another arcanist set a trap for Cherney."

Mika grabbed a bag from the pile and stepped away from us, facing the road to the west.

A large black SUV drove down the narrow street, a light flashing on the dashboard. The top of the windshield was dark, hiding all but the square chin of the man driving it. The FBI insignia on his jacket became clear as he drew nearer. The police had congregated at the entrance, appearing to be organizing the employees in evacuation, but they paused at the new arrival.

"Who's Aston's direct supervisor, Neddie?" Mika asked.

"McKenna. Isaac has been liaising with him."

As the SUV approached, Mika strode forward, keeping to the passenger side, but still bringing him to a stop. The police and employees glanced from us to Aston, even as the first civilian was urged to head down the building toward the road.

With a gesture for us to retrieve the rest of the pile, Mika opened the passenger side and slid into the seat next to Aston. The door closed, but we could hear them over the comms. "We've got a lead, but we need to move quickly."

Aston's hard face turned to stone as I carried the cooler and ammo box past his window. "Now look here. I've come down to get some answers on all this. We're getting the runaround about the actual details."

I reached the back of the vehicle, and Olivia opened the hatch while Mika answered. "That's McKenna's choice as to what he chooses to explain on the matter. I won't contradict his decision."

In the rearview mirror, Aston's frown loosened to a concerned fluster. "McKenna would tell me."

Mika pulled down the seatbelt. "He knows his team. I trust that. These are the coordinates. I'll put them in your navigation." Their fingers tapped on the dashboard screen as Aston sputtered, then Mika continued. "I appreciate him sending one of his best. We've got a potentially explosive situation on our hands."

Aston's head straightened, focusing on the crater behind the SUV. "Anyone hurt?"

"Oh yes, we've got casualties. Our people are on the way, but if you can spare someone for crowd control, it might save lives. Any of those vehicles could be rigged."

Voice gruff, though concerned, Aston made a call to get agents to the parking lot of the city's maintenance building and checked on others who might be available. Dagen had taken the seat behind Mika, so Olivia slid to the middle, leaving me behind Aston. Mika's intent expression appeared feigned, as if catered to Aston's experience. The sight made me uneasy.

When Aston finished, Mika thanked him. "We've got a lead on one of our targets, but I don't know for how long."

Aston put the car in drive, turning the wheel. "One of your targets?"

"Possibly the more dangerous of them."

I raised my eyebrows, scanning the lot where I'd nearly been mauled. *Not sure I agree.*

When we spun in a sharp turn, Olivia strained, careful not to bump her bandaged shoulder into me. I appreciated her concern.

Neddie spoke over the comms. "We've gotten nowhere on breaking the code, but we have tracked the comments to James Hilderbrand out of Phoenix. If it's any help, since he's already deceased."

My lips twitched, but I remained silent.

Mika put a hand to their earbud. "Thanks, Neddie." They twisted, studying me, as if waiting for some comment.

"Izzie, from my office, she's one of the best at breaking codes that I know of."

Mika smiled, and Neddie answered. "Izzie Forsythe. I'll check in with her. Any help I can get."

Aston, perhaps annoyed at being out of the conversation, punched the gas, flying down the narrow road. I'd grown accustomed to Olivia's careful precision at the wheel.

If the FBI mole hadn't alerted Cherney, I would have found the comments in time, and we might have been able to track them without all the deaths. Without losing everything.

I had no doubt we were heading into another trap and pulled up the map of the area where Neddie's report identified Cherney's burner. The Red Aegis had us dancing from one foot to the other, rather than on top of them. With Olivia watching, I zoomed in and out over a cozy residential neighborhood. The pinpointed location appeared to be a house, but triangulation could be off. I ran a search for the address. "It's an Airbnb."

"Yes," Neddie replied. "The information used to rent the house this morning was falsified. Prepaid card. The house is rented with a lockbox code, so the landlord never met anyone."

At least we knew the location was correct.

My phone buzzed with a message from my dad.

Funerals are set. Do you want to talk now or later?

I sagged, staring at the words. Olivia glanced at my face, then focused on the windshield.

With thick fingers, I typed a response. I'll call later.

CHAPTER

TWENTY-FIVE

For a brief second, my mind drifted with thoughts of Beth and Peter, funerals, and the pained family that would attend, then I shut them away. There would be words of sympathy and grief that I didn't want to face, though I would.

Twisted junipers grew in front of a wall on the west side of the street where a young man rode a red bike. From under his blue baseball cap, his pale brown ponytail hung over one shoulder of his dark, sweat-stained T-shirt. He passed us going the opposite way, leaving me to gaze unfocused at the blurs of traffic washed by the flashing blue of Agent Aston's dashboard light.

Olivia spoke in a quiet voice beside me. "The first time Cherney drew us in, he corralled us and attacked with blasting. The other Red Aegis tried to divide us and overwhelm us with portals. I am confident this is Cherney."

"As am I. He could have had plenty of time to rig the house, much like his home." I remembered Agent Todd and glanced at Aston's shoulders in the driver's seat. "We can expect him to lure us in. He might not even be inside, though." I frowned as Cherney would know of Haven detection spells. What did he have planned? Would he risk waiting inside as bait?

She watched me. "What?"

"Cherney has proved to be sharp. He will not just sit on a couch allowing us to trap him, but how will he lure us inside?"

Olivia didn't answer, and we slowed with traffic, Aston grumbling as he moved to the center suicide lane even though we approached a red light. I'd have preferred Olivia to be driving. After several seconds of weaving, honking, and a singular set of screeching tires, we made it through the intersection, nearly taking care of Cherney's problem for him.

Agent Aston answered his phone as we pushed over sixty on a clear stretch of the main road. "Yes, I want them pulled to my location. Both of them." He hung up, then turned to Mika. "I've got four agents meeting us. They're about fifteen minutes out, heading in from Mogul."

"Excellent. I appreciate McKenna putting you on this, Agent Aston."

I zoomed in on the neighborhood again to view the tight rows of houses twenty feet from their neighbors. We'd be risking others as well as ourselves, depending on what Cherney had planned.

A report arrived from Neddie with a simple diagram of our target house. A living room and kitchen shared the front of the residence, with bedrooms, baths, and a second exit at the back.

Aston drew my attention as he veered a sharp left, drawing a truck's braying horn. We pulled into the residential neighborhood, driving far too fast, and lurched over the first speed bump. He raced over another set even faster, and Olivia jostled into me, setting Tarus to unfurl beside me. After my day's experiences, it spiked my pulse.

"2725?" Aston asked.

"Yes," Mika answered.

I frowned, as that wasn't the address. As he took a corner, I noticed he wasn't on the correct street. Unsure of Mika's plan, I kept my mouth shut.

Mika pointed to parking on the right. "Pull in here. We'll set up in the rear, then our ops, Neddie, will link to your phone. Watch from out here and head for the front door when you get our call. They'll try to escape out the back."

He complied, clearing his throat. "Do you want to wait for backup?"

"Sounds good. It'll take us fifteen minutes to get into position. Neddie, can you connect with Agent Aston's phone?" Mika opened the passenger door. "Let us know if there's any movement."

I exited, followed by Olivia, while Dagen popped out the other side with Mika. Inside, I'd barely noticed the cool, but now the hot air stunk with baking asphalt and tires. A heavyset white man glanced at us from the shade of a large sumac where he worked under the hood of a battered pickup. Air conditioners hummed around us, and no one else had grown foolish enough to brave the midday heat. The light breeze offered no respite without shade. The beige, gray, and dirty-white houses of the neighborhood bore the brunt of time and too little money, while dried-out wooden fences carved up the spaces between buildings.

Led by Mika, we trotted across the street toward a gate between two residences, leaving Agent Aston cooling his heels, literally, in the FBI's SUV.

"What's the plan?" Mika asked as they sent a loop of a

Mer lifting spell into the fence. The latch clicked, and they opened the gate.

The resident had a sitting area set up with potted plants and an umbrella-covered round table, but the windows were tight with shades. The fence at the back leaned against a tree.

I closed the gate behind me, waiting to see who would answer, but Mika looked to me.

Olivia spoke. "If Cherney is setting us up, we can't determine how he'll try to get us to enter. We need to watch for his ambush."

"We're confident it's Cherney?" Mika asked, taking sure strides for the fence.

"The other arcanist wouldn't have had time to activate the phone to draw us in, even if they had access to it." Olivia glanced at me in confirmation and continued. "We know the burner isn't being used, but left on. The only other option I can see is that they have it available to receive a call or information, but I'd consider that a slim probability."

We reached the backyard, and Mika leaned down to peer through warped boards. "Zach, light it up."

With a tug at Haven, I drew a detection spell and lobbed it to the roof of the white house, just over the pale green fascia. A single person, male from the shape, stood at the kitchen side of the house near the middle, if I'd gauged Neddie's diagram correctly. The faint wisps of white moved in a motion that reminded me of someone washing their face.

The yard and house on the other side of the dividing fence appeared empty.

"I see someone's home," said Mika. "Check for wards." Before I could start, they began climbing over with Dagen quick to follow.

Dur-Alf glowed at the left corner of the building. "I've got a ward at the side." I scrambled up, the boards groaning under me. The back windows had heavy shades drawn, and the yard had a neglected sitting area among the dirt and dried weeds.

The man hadn't moved far from his original position, but he seemed to be drinking, head tilted back and arm up. Hardly the furtive movements I'd expected. What had I expected? *Cowering like a scared rat?*

As I crept toward the sigil, a tendril of Mer blue reached up to the roof and shifted a camera. Mika crouched two paces from me, watching, with Dagen appearing ready to pounce. Olivia knelt by the fence, eyes darting about.

With ease, I unraveled a binding ward by a side door, then nodded to Mika. They came to the corner. "Where is he?"

I pointed ten feet ahead at the first window. If we entered through this door, it would be heard. The man took a step, leaned with one arm moving as if opening a door, then reached as if pulling something from a fridge. It was lunchtime. Had Cherney just killed a number of people with cryptids, then come home for a snack?

Mika moved up close, peering at the edge of the window of the door as if trying to see past the shade there. "Dagen. Is it Cherney?"

"There's a whiff, but not strong." Dagen pressed her nose against the crack. "Not Cherney. Male."

My frown drew Mika's attention, but they smiled. "C'mon. Up front." They pointed across the rear of the building. "Dagen, Olivia. Be ready if we spook him out the back."

I tugged at my collar, reminding them of the Tarus portal that had been released from Lex Unger. As we padded quietly through the dirt and dried grass, I realized that Cherney had set a trap using the other Red Aegis by leaving his cell somewhere on the property. Mika had figured it out quickly. But where was Cherney?

As we turned the opposite corner, leaving the others guarding the rear, Mika shot another lifting spell up to the eaves, adjusting a camera near the front that overlooked the gate and front door. Tucked at the edge of a wide overhang, it now pointed to the beams there.

A distant dog barked in the neighborhood from somewhere to the west. The front fence, painted rust red, held a gate, over which I could make out the top of the carport. Concrete formed a path from the door, past a window and under worn boards. Two scrub junipers sat in decorative pots beside the door; one with dark soil spilled at its base appeared to have been tipped and righted .

With a gesture, I paused Mika, drew from Haven, and sent a detection spell over the fence to the neighbor's house. A single figure reclined near the front, as if watching television. Mika studied me. I pointed. "One person, but they seem to be resting. Where is Cherney? He set this up."

"Indeed. Maybe he just wants us to get rid of a problem."

I rubbed the stubble on my face, wishing it might be that simple. The blinds had been pulled on this side of the house as well, keeping the sun out and us hidden. The man inside sat now, eating. He'd set traps to kill people, then returned for lunch, even knowing he hadn't finished the job. Belatedly, I tugged at the realms.

Mika's eyebrows rose as three wards bloomed with dark green, one on the inside of the gate and two on the wall beside it, all blasting spells. He would have drawn the one on the gate from the inside, and an arcanist had to be very careful in disarming their sigils. It took skill that most didn't have.

My eyes went to the door. "He'll have warded the inside of the door, possibly both. He's good."

"Dagen, don't enter that door, no matter what." Mika stared at the entry. "Think he'll run if I open the door from here and set off whatever he has waiting?"

I watched the arcanist, eating and drinking, perhaps checking a phone from his movements. With two steps, I aligned the window between me and him. "I might be able to blast the window and hit him with a binding spell, if he's not wearing a binder's block."

"You lead; I'll follow. Once the door blows, I'll be moving in. Follow me. I want him alive." Mika did not draw their weapon.

"Would it be more effective if Dagen and Olivia could enter at the same time?" I asked.

"Yes."

"Hold on." I moved with quick steps, aiming for dirt rather than the random leaf or patches of weeds, and darted around the back to a surprised Olivia. "I'm going to set it up so you can blow the door. Keep back about ten feet."

Dagen's head popped around the corner as I arrived. "How?"

I dug from Dur-Alf and placed a blasting ward on the lower part of the door's window as I explained. "When you hear us breech, shoot the window from about four paces away. I've shaped it to blast in and down; that should set off any wards. Still, be careful."

Despite a growing weariness, I sent another detection spell against the wall where the man ate before moving to the other side and joining Mika. They would have heard my explanation over the comms, so I nodded toward our target. "Still eating at the table ahead."

We stood together about twelve feet from the window and eighteen from the door. As Mika drew in an unlocking spell and another for lifting, I tugged at Dur-Alf for mine. The breeze pushed through, doing little to cool me under the sun. Sharpened by the desire to capture just one of the Red Aegis, my mind ran through several possible scenarios.

TWENTY-SIX

I raised both hands, taking a deep breath within the sweat-soaked vest. Air conditioners whined from the houses of the neighbors we were about to rouse with our attack, but otherwise nothing seemed to stir in the stifling summer air.

Mika focused on the door.

"Here goes," I said.

My blast spell slapped against the middle of the window, but my eyes were trained on the Haven ghost of the figure seated at the table. He'd just raised his arm up and tilted his head for a sip when my explosion blew in the window.

The white shade shredded from glass and magic billowing inward. Then, one of his wards flashed up in mossy green, triggered by the blast, releasing a binding spell.

I paused in throwing my own binding as the released trap swirled toward the ceiling, blocking my aim.

Mer blue flashed to my right as Mika's unlocking spell sank into the door. *At that distance. Impressive.*

The man inside had fallen back in his chair, leaving me with yet another obstacle as the table now sat between us. I'd hoped he'd stand. I stepped forward with Dur-Alf pinched in my fingers at my shoulder, as if I might throw a dart.

In the rear, Dagen fired, and the ward I'd set on the back entrance shattered with the muffled clatter of wood and glass. I had to hope that, similar to the window, the man had set his wards close to the door, not a few steps inside.

He began to rise, but not high enough for me to have a clear shot at his upper body. One of his feet slipped, causing him to grab at the table. *Just stand*, I urged. My chest moved as I released a breath.

As Mika slung a lifting spell into the door and opened it, a blasting ward triggered on the inside with a spray of splinters, but I'd expected nothing less. The wards outside fired in a chain reaction, buckling the fence and banging the gate ajar. They did so with flying debris and a rush of air and sound, but without flame, typical of a Dur-Alf blasting spell. However, the pot that held the disturbed juniper exploded with a fiery center. *An actual bomb*. The resulting wall of pressure threw me off my feet.

Mika was slammed into me, and a splash of blue Mer colored my sight.

This is the trap. Pain radiated from my right temple before I struck the ground. With a grunt, I landed on my left shoulder. The momentum rolled my face into the dirt. I'd lost the binding spell. The hand that had held it lay twisted under my body, and sand stuck to my face.

"Mika?" Dagen yelled through the comms.

I can hear. To untangle myself, I flopped onto my back. Some shard had grazed my temple, bloodying my sweaty hair; my knee and elbow had been struck by debris as well, but they seemed more bruised than cut.

Dagen swore. "What the hell did you do, gym bro?" With measured breath and scuffing feet, she was hopefully moving in from the back with Olivia as she spoke. A grunt sounded over the comms.

As I leaned up on my elbow, I could make out a snarl of bodies where our target had been. Beside and behind me, Mika rose with a bleeding hand.

"Give it up, you little—" Dagen's voice cut off, and I shoved myself to my knees.

Mika, despite multiple wet spots growing in their suit, dragged themselves up and paused to offer me a hand. Their face had a nasty gash on the cheek that trailed blood to the chin. "Okay?" they asked me.

Dust or smoke clouded the house, but the door and overhang were gone along with a bite out of the wall the size of a washing machine; it extended the entry nearly to the far window. The fence lay flat, exposing the street and neighbors' homes on the opposite side.

"Think so," I muttered. "That was explosive."

With no comment necessary, Mika moved toward the enlarged doorway, though fire kindled just inside.

In the dining area, the faint white figures had ceased moving, with one nearly standing, perhaps on another. I wiped away blood before it reached my eye and forced my legs to follow.

"Prisoner secured," said Olivia, with none of the satisfaction that the rest of us might have intoned.

I admired her. My first reaction was to mention the Tarus suicide ward that the target might have, but she'd have considered it. With a pained hint of a smile, I kept my mouth shut.

"Suppress that," Mika said, pointing to the fire and moving with growing speed into the house.

My hand paused in my hair. "How?" Baseboard and carpet had caught, burning reluctantly.

"Phistrel used a shield, pressed tight to remove the air. Thank you."

I tugged a spell out, noting my waning energy, and did as she suggested. It worked. *Something new. Not a skill I'd needed — until now.*

The planter, where I assumed the bomb had been, no longer existed. Its counterpart lay scattered in a pile with a ruined Juniper.

Dagen had said there'd been a whiff of Cherney. *He planted the bomb.*

The door, the largest remaining bit of it, rested against a credenza on the far wall. Books and a toppled bookshelf spread across the floor to my right. In the dining area ahead of me, Olivia had the man's wrists locked in one hand, his arms twisted nearly perpendicular at the shoulders, and her boot on the base of his spine. In her free hand, she took pictures of his face. *A handsome face.*

Behind both of them curled Dagen. I frowned as Mika stepped between us, blocking my view. Our werewolf hadn't moved, and I'd just realized it. Against the wall, her extended nails reached forward, as if attempting to grasp the air. Her teeth gritted in a short muzzle, and her eyes were locked on me.

I tugged at Dur-Alf, lighting up the binding that wove around her. Careful not to smile, I stepped closer beside Mika and released Dagen. She unwound like a striking snake from where she'd fallen to her side and spat out a string of curses. As she stood, her hand raised as if to strike the prisoner, and I expected Mika to say something, but Dagen just made a fist and marched away.

Our target had a young, petite face with short peach-colored hair and green eyes with a hint of dark blue. He stared at Mika, who gave me a nonchalant gesture to bind him, so I did. The spell took without resistance. *No binder's block.*

In an exasperated voice, close to the tone she'd used with me when we first met, Neddie spoke over the comms. "Aston's moving. Couldn't stop him. I believe he has others aimed for you as well."

Mika swore and gestured to me with a bloodstained hand.

I took a faltering step for the door, tugging at the realms to check for wards or coins. My body shook, distressed in the aftermath. "Stay away from the windows," I said as sigils glowed. While I got my legs under me and walked, I pulled from Haven and, as I exited into an acrid haze, tossed it to the front of the neighbor's house. As expected, the lone figure had risen, but hovered near the wall as if peeking through a window.

After stepping across the fractured fence, I removed a ward from the concrete under the carport and a second at the edge of the street. The small Toyota parked there had no sigils, inside or out. A breeze carried the charred smell around the corner, but I welcomed it and the momentary shade.

The revving engine of Aston's SUV preceded his squeal of tires as he took the corner. His type would be livid at being misled. With casual steps, I moved to the asphalt.

Two neighbors had braved the sun and stood alone with their phones recording the scene. I smeared some of the blood spatters across my face, attempting to wipe them away, then checked my ego. With a more paranoid scan, I searched the houses and streets for any signs of Cherney. *He brought us here.*

I pointed for Agent Aston to park in the center of the street, in front of the house next door. Instead, he stopped at my toes. Red-faced, he glared at me as he opened his door.

"What kind of bullshit is this?" he demanded.

"Wrong house. Our mistake," Mika prompted over the comms.

I parroted her words with a shrug.

He swore, but his eyes flicked from my blood to the ruined fence at the front, and he didn't attempt to head inside. "What happened?"

"Explosives on premises. Two-block cordon." Mika's voice, calm and relaxed, eased the tension, at least for me.

I shifted away from the heat of his running car since I already stood in the full sun. "Our target has explosives stashed on the property. We're bringing in people to deal with it. Agent Mika wants a two-block cordon around the house."

"Where is he? Inside? I need to speak to him."

"*They*," I enunciated with weight, "are securing the premises. What we can't have is someone setting off any more of the munitions. We've contained the fire."

He eyed the smoke. His lips twitched as though preparing another argument, but he just stormed away without a word, returning to his air conditioning.

Over the comms came Dagen's grumblings and then Mika spoke. "Everek, I need you."

"I'm helping Yasmine. We just reached the maintenance facility." His voice wavered between low and high pitches.

"Want me have the locals take some?" asked Yasmine over the comms.

"We can't release the victims to locals, not with the wounds."

"Fine, boss. Get me a semi with a freezer."

Mika chuckled. "Not. Body bag them. Secure them. Have the FBI put them on ice. I need Everek here. Sorry."

In the following silence, I kept wary, even starting when Dagen came out, boots crunching on boards. She paced in a circle around me before speaking, twirling her finger about. "Oh, and thanks again." Her mouth curved at the corners. "We bagged a live one."

I assumed her gesture implied a binding, and my lips pursed. "Technically two." With a tentative smile, I pointed at her.

Dagen grinned when she punched my shoulder.

Agent Aston stepped out of his car with a calmer demeanor. "We've got more people heading over. I'm going to secure these four corners around this block first. We'll widen when we get manpower."

"He sounds almost polite," said Mika over the comms. "Isaac must have gotten some weight involved."

"Thank you," I said to Aston, who nodded a bit too much before marching toward the south end of the street.

"Lily in five minutes," reported Neddie.

With the FBI arriving to cordon the streets, I relaxed my hypervigilance and moved to stand in the shade of the carport. My scalp stung, dulled from the initial pain, while my elbow had grown a solid knot.

With little noise, Olivia padded across the fallen gate, eyes darting to our audience, which had increased to three with a lone man and a pair of women. "You should clear the house and . . ." she trailed off as she motioned to her collar.

I'd considered it, but Aston had decided to join us. "I'll do that now."

Dagen paced while Olivia watched the street as I headed back inside.

I'd left the young man, close to my age, with his arms stretched back, assuming the others would reposition him. *That's got to be uncomfortable.* A normal binding as I'd used left all autonomic responses intact, such as breathing, but the muscles would lock in place, requiring someone to manually move them. They'd give without being harmed.

Mika sat at the table with their phone and glanced up, curious.

I pointed to our target, then tugged at the realms. Nothing. Body straight and arms pulled back, he appeared as if in a dive, despite the linoleum in his face. With a firm but gentle press, I lowered his arms, then rolled him over.

Soda had soaked into the front of his gray worker's uniform, and a piece of fried chicken strip lay flattened on the floor. His handsome face appeared distorted from pressing against the linoleum. I tugged, but no realms glowed on his clothes. "He's clear. Let me get the rest of the house."

"Not quite what we expected, was it?" Mika asked.

I moved past, unraveling the ward behind them on the kitchen window. "Not at all. We seem to be underestimating them."

"Agreed. Everything okay outside?"

As I passed again, heading for the intact window at the side near the front, I replied, "I keep expecting Cherney to appear on the roof, tossing coins."

"Good to be vigilant." Mika lifted their phone to read, seeming almost relaxed.

My next check was the laundry room, where my blast had dented the dryer. Whatever traps had been waiting were gone. I moved to the bedrooms and bathrooms, clearing windows. After the explosion and capture, the silence in the house and comms proved unnerving. An attack immediately afterward would almost have been more welcome than the quiet. On one bed, I found a backpack, which I checked before picking up.

Whoever we'd caught had barely used the place, but he was screwed on the deposit.

Over the comms, Olivia and Dagen greeted someone, and I hurried to finish disarming the last two windows. Our captured tenant had been very diligent.

A young feminine voice echoed over the comms from the living room. "Where is this new one that Yasmine is talking about?"

TWENTY-SEVEN

I stepped into the relative warmth of the main room where the blowing vents fought against the gaping entry.

The air smelled of pine and spice, maybe incense, and a young woman stood just inside the entrance, large eyes trained on me. Her black hair hung braided to her waist, and she had rich brown skin highlighting an oval face. I would have guessed her to be about sixteen, but no teen could have snuck in past Olivia and Dagen. She wore a tight tank top, pale blue shorts, and sandals.

"Lily, I presume?" Some, my coworker Izzie for one, had a near-religious fascination with dragon-shifters. I did not.

"I'm impressed with your redecorating." With a wry smile, she stepped forward, inspecting me.

"Can't take the credit. Cherney rigged some explosives."

She shook my hand, releasing a flood of the liquid gold Salmhalla realm around her sandals and noting my reserved reaction. "Housewarming gift?"

I allowed myself a light smile in return. "Unfortunately."

"Pleasure to meet you, Zach Graves." Lily spun on her heel to stride toward our bound prisoner, who stared at the ceiling. She righted a chair and sat at his side, overlooking him. "Release him," she said with a sigh, and I stepped forward to comply. The light, young voice turned heavier with overlapping notes. "Who are you?"

A shiver crawled down my spine before I could pluck apart my binding. My thoughts grew muddy, attempting to analyze what she'd done. There had been no glimmer of Salmhalla, so she hadn't used the realm for a spell.

The moment I released him, the man spoke, then pulled away from Lily. "Tucker Kennedy." His words were hurried, with rising panic.

"Sit, little monkey." Lily's strange tone drew another chill across my arms. "Have you facilitated the access or opening to the Tarus realm?"

"Yes." He answered before he even righted himself, positioning himself cross-legged in front of her with stiff, reluctant movements.

Mika smiled and returned their attention to their phone. Blood stained the table where their sleeves had rested.

"Are you of the Red Aegis?" Lily asked.

"Yes."

"Who else of the Red Aegis is in Reno presently?"

"Michael Cherney, Matt Fahne, Jay Werner, James Hilderbrand, and Lex Unger."

Enchanted by the voice and situation, I broke free and stepped forward. "Michael Cherney is the last of them alive."

Mika's eyes raised and their head cocked, studying me.

Lily did not turn or rebuke me. "Is what he says true?"

"Yes, Michael Cherney is alive."

Emboldened, I drew a deep breath and spoke. *So many questions.* "Why are you trying to kill each other? Are you from different triads?"

Focus locked on Lily, Kennedy did not glance at me, but his jaw tightened.

"Answer him," Lily prompted.

Kennedy's speech faltered as he fought the hold she had on him, but he spoke. "In an unwise attack on Zach Graves, James Hilderbrand, one of my triad, assisted his liaison from the Shaper Triad, Michael Cherney. Lex Unger, of my triad, and I decided that they had become a potential risk to the organization and dedicated ourselves to eliminating both of them. Jay Werner and Matt Fahne, also of the Shaper Triad, confronted us in support of Michael Cherney."

Unwise? Peter and Beth had been murdered. I took a step forward. Fahne had died by my hand because of Cherney. Over ten innocents had died. Kennedy and Unger had likely been the drivers who killed Werner, but why set a trap for the DRC?

"Why did you set the Tarus traps at the maintenance building and the gas company?" I snapped out the question through a tight jaw.

Lily's multilayered tone rang in my ears. "Answer him."

Kennedy trembled. "Our primary goal is the eradication of the Consociation's rule of humanity."

"At what cost?" I growled.

With a gentle turn, Lily addressed me in her normal light voice. "I believe you've received answers that will help you address some of their activities. That is good. Do you have a final question before I continue?"

My face flushed. In my department, my previous department, I had a reputation for being strong-headed, and for the most part, my supervisors encouraged it, but at the moment, I'd let my emotions drive me. "Thank you. Does he have any information that might lead us to Cherney?"

She smiled before turning to Kennedy. "What do you know of Michael Cherney that might help us locate him?"

The man grimaced, as if trying to resist. "All Red Aegis prepare for the Consociation's eventual attack. He will have at least two vehicles hidden about the city that are registered and insured to people who cannot be traced to him. We know how deep your tendrils reach. He will have a list of campgrounds, hostels, and rooms that he can rent for cash or prepaid cards, both in the city and afar. Since you have identified him, he has chosen to offer himself as oblation, and will hunt you to your deaths, or his." Kennedy's upper lip rose in a grinning snarl. "You do not need to search for him; he will find you."

When he finished, Mika gestured for me to leave with an encouraging smile. "Let them know to be on guard, Zach."

I didn't think Olivia or Dagen needed to be reminded, but I had disrupted Lily's interrogation, for the little it had done. With a quick nod, I remained silent and turned to the remnants of the opening.

The Shaper Triad. Did they all have names? How many triads were there? My teeth ground, wanting the answers from Kennedy.

As I exited, Lily's weighty voice continued behind me. "What activities was your triad engaged in to further the Red Aegis agendas?"

I'd at least confirmed the rumor that the dragon-shifters could compel. I doubted that Kennedy would have answered any questions otherwise, and certainly not as thoroughly. As I stepped into the sun, I squinted against the glare. The sharp scent from the burning carpet and explosives lingered. If innocents hadn't died, I might not have cared that the triads turned on each other over my family's murder. *James Hilderbrand.* Why had he agreed to help Cherney if they weren't in the same triad?

As I ambled toward the road, or perhaps the cooler shade of the carport, Olivia watched me from the street. The comms were quiet, so Mika must have shut theirs off for the interrogation as I could barely hear Kennedy's voice through the opening.

Dagen paced near Aston's SUV, veering toward me as I stepped out of the beating sun onto the cracked and weathered concrete. "What do you think about Lily?" she asked.

I shrugged. "Young."

Dagen scoffed. "Hardly. You meet a lot of dragon-shifters in your previous gig?"

With my head tilted, I shook it slowly. "Read several of their reports, though." That wasn't a conversation I could have with anyone outside of my department. *My old department.* Had I moved on?

I nudged my chin toward the neighborhood. "Where do you suppose Cherney's hiding?"

My question drew Olivia as Dagen waved their hands up to her shoulders in an exaggerated shrug. "Beats me. He had a good opportunity when we were dealing with the big boom. I really thought that had been you."

"Perhaps," said Olivia, "Cherney is waiting for us to transport Tucker Kennedy, dead or alive, or the fullness of his plan was the explosive. I have been considering this question."

With a languid stroke, I rubbed my stubble while scanning the neighborhood. Our audience had doubled to six, though all were on the far side of the street and had retreated to the shade of trees or overhangs, making them more difficult to spot.

What is Cherney planning? I braved the brutal sun and walked toward Aston's car, tugging at the realms, but no sigils were on the sides or front. There were figures in dark jackets at either end of the road, FBI, guarding the corners, one beside a dark SUV similar to Aston's. When I frowned, my temple twinged.

"Everek's clearing the FBI," said Neddie.

Olivia had followed two steps behind, and we both turned toward the end where we expected him to turn. "You need to get that looked at. I believe you've lost a lot of blood."

With a tentative probe, my fingers pressed against matted hair that began at my temple and continued behind my ear. The slice had started at the hairline, but dug about two inches back. I smeared blood on my neck and tugged the collar of my T-shirt, but the vest held it tight.

Six inches lower, and it might have sliced my neck. "I guess so."

"I got you," said Everek, pitch low on the comms. In a county maintenance truck, he turned at the corner, the FBI agent there waving him through.

Dagen bounded to the rear of Aston's SUV. "What are you driving?"

"The only thing they agreed to let the FBI sequester. I've got a traffic signal in the back." He sounded amused.

Our audience had grown interested in the new arrival, heads turning at his approach. Dagen leaned against Aston's car, waiting.

As Everek pulled to the side to park in front of us, a blasting spell ripped apart his front tire and buckled the adjacent panel with a groan. I stiffened. I'd checked the immediate area, but not that far down. Steam and smoke poured from the engine while it rattled to its death.

Mika's comm popped on. "What happened?"

As I ran toward the car with Olivia, I answered. "Blasting ward. Everek hit one." The truck leaned to its side and forward, as if wounded. My eyes snapped to the closest of the watching spectators, but the woman only fumbled at her cell for a picture. From two houses down at the corner where he'd arrived, she had a clear view.

Dagen had already sprinted to Everek's door and yanked it open. "He's okay." She too, glanced about, expecting an attack from a nearby house.

Everek exited, hat in hand. "Yeah, bit surprised is all." Even his illusion appeared stunned, wearing a frown.

Olivia and I slowed to a jog, snapping wary glances about. At the south end where Everek had turned onto the street, the FBI agent remained at his position but watched us. Antifreeze seeped from the engine as I tugged at the realms, searching the area for more hidden sigils or curse coins.

"I'll be right out." Mika sounded rushed, already in motion.

Everek and Dagen moved to the curb as Olivia and I stopped in front of the ruined maintenance truck. With my hand shading my eyes, I scanned the house next to where Kennedy had been residing, then the other side, sure that we could expect an attack.

Mika leaped over the fence, then slowed, appraising the situation.

My eyes lingered, first on the car parked in the drive, then to the carport, before snapping to the odd shape on the top. It could have been someone's discarded jacket. A whitish-gray lump resembled a bag, ruffling under the light breeze.

Cherney had lured us here, likely hoping that the first explosion might kill some of us. He'd have more waiting, though. *A second bomb.* Maybe one he could control remotely.

Lily stepped onto the flattened fence, drawing Mika's attention, who stopped at the edge of the carport to turn. The second explosive could be built with shrapnel and made to take out responders. Even Olivia and I might be within that range.

"Move away from the house. Bomb." My voice firm, it caused Mika to swing toward me and brought Lily to a halt.

As I pointed above them, it only spread confusion. Lily glanced behind, over the toppled fence and into the yard, with Mika following her search rather than knowing that danger might be right overhead.

I took a step toward them, then stopped and dug for a shield. Mika risked the most, and I could at least protect them, if not the rest of us.

From the far end of the street to the north, a short burst of fully automatic gunfire rattled off three, maybe four rounds.

There, some eighty yards away, the FBI agent who'd been guarding the corner crumpled to the street.

A lone figure turned the muzzle of the weapon toward us. *Cherney.*

TWENTY-EIGHT

I gauged the distance between us and Cherney and considered the shield I held ready. Olivia and I stood in the middle of the street with Dagen at the edge; at this range, getting hit would require bad luck. Where Mika stood, head cocked and too close to the possible explosive, there was less danger of being shot, but a serious risk if a bomb waited on the carport.

With a flick, I sent the shield to spread in a thin wall between Mika and the carport. "Bomb!" I repeated.

Dagen swore as Olivia leaped forward, running toward the machine gun toting figure, then our werewolf growled with deepening levels as she sprinted to follow.

As I reached for another shield, Lily backed over the fence, away from the shield protecting Mika.

Cherney shifted and fired.

A torrential burst rattled from his weapon. Everek's ruined work truck clanged with a pair of hits while one bullet ricocheted off the asphalt at my toes.

Olivia twisted and toppled to the road, falling on her

bandaged shoulder and rolling twice before catching herself. Dagen passed her, untouched.

I felt intact and checked Mika, who had started to move down the street before the gunfire. They took a step, faltered, and grabbed their leg before stumbling to the asphalt. My eyes flicked to Cherney, already fleeing toward the houses behind him and a freeway upon the slope beyond them. *Stop him, Dagen.* I had to get Mika away from the bomb.

Mika saw me turning and yelled. "Go. Go!"

A moment's pause on my part left me in the middle of the road when the explosive tore apart the carport. A wooden beam the thickness of my arm scraped against the top of my shield before somersaulting in front of my face. *One step more.* I staggered from the blast and debris, but kept on my feet.

The small sedan, its roof crumpled, burst into flames.

Mika, who had stepped to the edge of my shield toward Cherney before being shot, skidded to the middle of the street and remained motionless.

Blood dripped from my hand where an inch-long shard was impaled in the outer edge. I'd lost the shield I'd prepared.

I moved for Mika, but Everek's voice came from behind. "I've got them. Get him."

Ahead, halfway down the street, Dagen sprinted, and I took off after her.

Olivia had been hit in the upper thigh but had pushed herself up to one knee. Her focus remained on the row of houses Cherney had darted between. The tops of trucks rumbled on the highway above the two buildings where he'd disappeared. *He can't cross that easily.*

"Dagen, he'll have set traps. Wait for me." I listened for some response from her over the comms.

She huffed, but didn't speak and didn't slow down.

I raced across the asphalt, sneakers scuffing at forty yards behind her and losing ground. "We have him penned in." In truth, I doubted that, but didn't want her stepping on a blast ward.

The homes where Cherney had fled had one car in the carport but no sign of curious residents. Any oglers on our street had vanished from sight at the gunfire and explosion. I passed a car on my left, rear windshield shattered from a bullet.

"Dagen?" I asked as she dashed recklessly onto a dry lawn and under the shade of a pair of trees.

Beside his car, the FBI agent lay face up on the street in a pool of shiny blood. He'd parked to block the corner.

Unlike the house we'd helped blow up, many beside the highway were two stories and backed up the slope that led to the guardrails. From the brush and power lines, the hill continued on the far side of the traffic. I could hear the trucks easily as I approached.

As I neared the corner and the downed agent, I tugged at Dur-Alf, quickly spotting scattered coins that Dagen had navigated through. At her speed, she'd have reached the highway by now. "Dagen?"

I tugged a detection spell from Haven as I reached the three-way intersection and tossed it between the buildings. With heavy breaths, I danced past the coins and reached the grass. One ghost-white figure showed at the window, peeking through the curtains.

Another one, motionless like a statue, waited at the back.

I jumped atop a fence that divided the houses, leg and arm dangling over the side while tugging at the realms in caution. Dagen's bound form, angled in full stride, lay at the corner of the house upon some gravel. Cherney did not show up in my detection spell.

"Clear?" asked Olivia over the comms. She'd reached the FBI agent.

"Coins." My voice husky from running, I swallowed as I leaped the fence. "Dagen's back here. No sign of Cherney."

A small dog chirped from inside the residence, attempting to guard it.

The backyard climbed a steep incline to the rose-colored sand and brush at the edge of the highway. Beyond the top of a passing truck, I couldn't make out anything up there.

I checked the path once more before reaching Dagen and pulling the binding free for the third time that day. She snapped out of it with a snarl, swearing a stream.

As Olivia climbed the fence, fettered by her wounded leg, I glanced back. Blood soaked her slacks, as it had her sleeve. *Tough.*

From above, a familiar burst of gunfire rained over us. I spun to the muzzle fire from the cover of the brush at the highway's edge twenty yards away. The first punch of a bullet hit me in the upper chest, and it felt like I imagined a heart attack would. Shocked by the sensation, my brain took a moment to resolve Dagen's cry, the chipping concrete and plaster, and the demolition of a window at the rear.

As the burst, no more than three seconds, finished, a second punch hit me high in the chest, nearly at the shoul-der. My mouth opened to take a breath, but my lungs rebelled.

Dagen had taken at least one hit in her calf, based on the blood, but her hands pressed at her side.

I staggered, breathless, and checked on Olivia, who

showed no signs of being shot beyond being slightly slower than usual.

We can't lose him. My lips peeled from my teeth as I forced myself to inhale. Eyes locked on the ridge above, I stumbled forward. "Dagen?" I croaked.

She waved me on. Cool air wafted out of the house, smelling of weed. The dog had retreated deeper inside but continued its barking.

With a last-minute caution, I tugged at the realms, securing a ready shield, then climbed the fence, groaning the whole way. My bones ached as if they were broken, but I doubted I'd be moving if they were. *I'm not losing him.*

Olivia moved slowly behind me. "He could be reloading."

I lifted my fingers with a spell she couldn't see, but didn't speak. The steep angle of sand crumbled under my sneakers while I steadied with one hand, watching the bushes at the top. Both relief and frustration grew as someone, Cherney, turned an ignition, but it didn't fire. My words came out in tempo with staggered footsteps. "He's got a vehicle." Of course he did.

"License plate?" Neddie asked, surprising me.

"We can't see," replied Olivia from behind.

Despite how sheer the angle had turned, I tugged at the realms, searching for a trap. The traffic sounded close enough to touch. As I climbed into the brush, it smelled of mesquite, baked under a cruel sun, and the ground blessedly eased its slant.

The car failed again; an older white van based on the roof. My finger touched a spent shell dropped in the sand, but I ignored it, moving in a quickening frenzy. "We can't let him escape."

The engine coughed to a start as I planted my first level footstep of the climb and tore through the thigh-high brush. Cars raced down the highway, ignoring the decrepit van and me. A semi roared past in the closest of two east-bound lanes, gusting me with dust and wind.

Cherney had parked along the busy road at the end of a guardrail. Scraped and dented paint revealed glimpses of dull or rusted metal beneath. When he shifted into gear with a thud, my pulse sped.

I sent a shield in front of the van in an attempt to block him in. As fast, I dug a lifting spell from Mer to tug at the door handle, assuming he'd climbed in from this side. It opened.

His vehicle jerked forward, smacking into my shield, but my placement had been off center, closer to me, forcing the nose of the van into traffic.

A long and persistent beep screeched from behind. By then I had almost reached the open door with Olivia nearing my shoulder.

Cherney bucked the van free of my shield and lurched into the road.

A streaking beep ending with a shrieking clash of metal as a blue blur slammed into the side of the van before veering into the next lane. There, it clipped a black truck, shiny and new, before spinning out of my sight.

The van's back tires kicked stone and dirt as Cherney punched the gas. With a futile gesture, I slapped the side to produce a hollow thud.

Olivia called out the numbers of the license plate to Neddie while I panted and glared after the escaping vehicle.

I watched Cherney escape, the van wobbling slightly as he picked up speed. Sweat drenched my clothes, and a vice pinched my chest. The small blue sedan, crumpled on both sides like a spent beer can, spun to a stop in the middle of both lanes.

Rubber squealed as a lifted red pickup with oversized tires stopped in the far lane. A rebel flag poked up from behind the cab, rustling in the breeze.

"Can we commandeer a vehicle?" I asked Olivia, but I was already running.

She kept pace, producing her badge.

The blond-haired man in the driver's seat wore a baseball cap that matched the color of his paint job. A cheap rifle hung on a gun rack behind his head.

We darted around the back of his vehicle, catching his attention in the mirror so that he was not completely surprised when we moved to his door. From the disdainful, entitled glare he gave us and Olivia's badge, I knew this kind of jerk from a lifetime of experience. Close to my age, his pink face seemed prone to a scowl that enhanced his scorn as he moved slowly for the button to roll his window down.

No time. I unlocked his door with a spell while readying a lifting spell. My lips twitched with satisfaction as the lock clicked and I flung open his door. With my magic, I shifted his car into park, increasing his growing shock. Already breaking a few Consociation rules, I reached over his lap unseen and unbuckled his seatbelt. His mouth dropped as the buckle slid across him.

"FBI. Get out, we're commandeering this vehicle." I had to at least look as if I was being reasonable, for Olivia's sake.

This, as expected, raised his hackles, and shook him from his surprise. "Like hell you will." He added a few more choices curses while reaching for his door.

A lifting spell has an element that witches learn in school. It can ride in your hand, so when I gripped his extended arm, I also had the strength of Mer attached to it.

His eyes widened as I yanked him halfway out of his cab with one arm, pausing a brief second so his feet could shuffle into position. His height matched my five-foot-eleven, but he carried an extra twenty pounds above my weight. With apparent ease, I spun him with two hands out of the truck, set him on the ground, and pressed him to sit on the median. My chest screamed from the strain, still complaining about the bruises under the vest.

In the hustle, the driver had lost his hat, and the wind whipped it into the traffic on the other side of the highway.

The entire process of unlocking his door and scooping him out took less than sixty seconds, though Cherney's van grew distant. Olivia already scrambled across the seat to the passenger side.

Before the blond-haired man caught his wind to start

swearing again and collected his nerve, I shot inside and had slammed the door.

"Sorry," I said to Olivia.

Her eyes studied my face as we buckled up. "For what?"

I dropped the roid-enlarged pickup into drive and stomped the gas, keeping a sharp eye that the owner didn't get himself entangled. He punched the rear panel. I maneuvered another lifting spell into opening the back window of the cab. As we picked up speed, I glanced at the rearview mirror, plucked the confederate flag out of its holder, and tossed it to the road. We passed the driver of the crumpled blue sedan with Cherney barely visible downhill.

Olivia focused on Cherney, speaking over the comms as I hoped Neddie worked with locals to join the chase. He'd already gone through the green light of an intersection ahead of us, and I was nearing sixty to catch up.

The signal turned yellow. *Crap.* Right foot pressed to the floor, I rolled down my window, letting the dry air gust over us like a vengeful banshee. I pulled a shield from Dur-Alf with my left hand and jabbed my thumb on the horn while steering. We'd be flying through on the red. Cherney would likely notice.

Without a hint of concern, Olivia pointed to a silver sports car lined up to our right, waiting to cross. "Watch out for that one."

In an abundance of caution, I sent the shield ahead of us to form in front of the revving potential threat. The light turned red, and as she'd suspected, the little silver car lurched forward, perhaps not seeing or hearing us. Either way, we blew through the intersection with horns blaring and a dumbfounded college kid trying to figure out why his tires had squealed but he was stuck in place. It would take a while for the spell to fade on its own; a massive fail in the eyes of the Consociation, but I guessed there wouldn't be much in the way of consequences, considering everything else that had gone on today. *Don't really care.*

Cherney had over a hundred yards on me, but I was eating up the distance. He'd passed a white sedan, nearly as dilapidated as his van, and pulled into the right lane in front of it.

"I've got a local patrol car coming onto McCarran from 395. They'll be behind you if your target remains on course." Over the comms, Neddie spoke in a fast, sharp voice.

Mika, their tone duller than usual, spoke. "I am taking one of the FBI's vehicles. Neddie is setting me up a route to join you."

My eyes flicked to Olivia. *We had this.* The main road slanted down to another intersection, already red. "Approaching a red light. Cherney's probably going to turn right. He's likely spotted me."

The little sedan ahead of us veered into my lane as the asphalt erupted in front of it. *A curse coin.*

"I would agree that he knows," said Olivia.

I pulled to the left of the white car as it swerved and skidded to try to stop. The pickup's large tires ate up the median with barely a bump as I flattened two yellow warning cones. We rumbled past without losing any speed, and I lurched back onto the asphalt.

Unsure of the consequences, I readied a blasting spell of my own. *Got to stop him somehow.* Twenty-five yards behind him, I trailed his van in the same lane, preparing to throw.

This close, the handful of coins tossed out of his window were like a spray of clay confetti. I could see Cherney's jet black hair and mustache as he grinned in his side mirror.

So far, he'd used blasting and binding, whereas others had opened Tarus. I couldn't take the chance. If I directed my blasting spell into them, then I could ignite most of them before we were too close, but what if he sent a handful of coins to trigger portals?

I dismissed my spell without hesitation and picked out a shield instead. As I spun it forward, I maneuvered it to match the descent of the clustered coins and the speed of the beast that I drove. To my right, a heavy concrete barrier protected the shoulder, and the monster tires might try to climb it, but I veered into the breakdown lane anyway.

My shield formed a wide bowl, collecting the clay tokens as they dropped. I held my breath as I shifted them down, close to the asphalt. Focused, I jumped when the right corner of the truck scraped sparks off the cement sections, screeching like a smashed guitar.

I passed my shield, easing it over the barrier to the dirt behind us. "We'll have to come back for those," I said to Olivia.

As I'd expected, Cherney turned right, but we were a couple hundred yards short of the intersection. Cherney had pulled into a turn lane in front of a Sonic at around forty miles per hour. His van tilted with the effort of turning at such a quick speed, and we were on course for his bumper.

Still in the breakdown lane, I slammed on the brakes, both hands on the wheel. My tires bucked as I aimed to stop beside the turn lane rather than rear-end him.

Anyone else would have had the oh-shit handle or dashboard in hand, but Olivia just leaned with the deceleration, her eyes on the van.

Cherney didn't make the turn; instead, at the last second, he whipped his wheels straight and rode up the sidewalk. The old van wobbled as the first tire took the curb, then reared as it ran down the stop sign at the driveway.

"We've got him." I wasn't surprised to find a smile tugging at my cheeks. Even in the tire-squealing throes of braking, I pulled my foot off the pedal and slammed it onto the gas, aiming to ram the front of the van. "Hold on," I told Olivia.

As Cherney's van scraped over the sign, its back doors blew open with the mossy-green of Dur-Alf; the midnight mist of Tarus bloomed as if an unfolding thunderstorm had fallen out of the rear.

THIRTY

Teeth gritted, I jerked the steering wheel so that we jumped onto the curb, missing the growing portal but clipping the back of Cherney's van. We had to stop and deal with whatever came out of Tarus. *We have to.*

The impact lurched the van forward, and for a brief, hopeful moment I thought it might tip on the slight incline, but he just swerved off the sidewalk and swale to drive into the parking lot. Olivia already had her seatbelt unbuckled, and I had to stop. As the truck's tires slid to a halt on dry grass and sand, I watched the broken van lumber down the embankment toward the front of a tire store, rear doors swinging, one on a single hinge.

"Tarus portal at our location," Olivia said as she threw open her door.

With one hand releasing the buckle, I drew a blasting spell with the other and leaned out of my window to throw it.

A shrill scream wailed from Olivia's side of the truck, and I moved in haste to send my spell into the side of

Cherney's vehicle. Even as it blasted at his door, I had mine open, jumping out to help Olivia. I'd wasted a moment, either in a thirst for vengeance or frustration that we might lose him yet again.

"Olivia?" I called out.

The van slammed into a car parked at the tire store, but I had to dash for the back of the truck as she failed to reply. The dark mist of the Tarus portal had disappeared. In its place stood a void roughly in the shape of a human. *Spectre. Shadow person.*

There had been reports of them, but beyond rare.

This one had appendages of dark emptiness touching the sides of Olivia's head. *Had that been her scream?* She stood with a limp, unresisting posture. Her gun remained in her holster.

Without much thought, I dug into Dur-Alf for a binding. I might catch her. I'd adjust it if I did. The distance between me and them measured less than six feet, so the spell hit the void in the center of its mass, or absence of one.

The black void rippled, swallowing the mossy green binding. My spine chilled, faced with something I didn't know how to stop.

The spectre released Olivia, and the scream definitely emanated from it. Somehow, I knew this faceless nothing had turned its focus on me.

Olivia stumbled back, sucking in a shuddering breath as she slapped against the side of the truck.

I retreated a step. "What stops it?" Gravel scuffed under the heel of my sneaker. My fingers reached for the realms, one hand drawing a shield, the other reaching for the comfort of an illusion.

As a youth, Mer had been my favorite of the realms, and I'd tended toward mischief on occasion. I took a step back, leaving a replica of myself standing motionless.

With a screech, the spectre took the bait, stretching tendrils of void to my illusory head but finding nothing to hold on to.

"Stops what?" asked Neddie.

I had no idea whether a shield would hold it, but I was willing to try. A crushing spell seemed useless in dealing with a cryptid that had no mass. Mika's method of extinguishing the fire earlier gave me inspiration.

Three feet away from the entity, I wrapped it like a burrito in my shield.

"A spectre," I finally answered, watching the void with growing trepidation.

It lacked any substance to tell me if it resisted, and the shield silenced it. As the seconds finally ticked away and the void remained within, I took a breath.

"Shoot it. Mercury or silver. Return it to Tarus." Neddie snapped out the list, though it had taken her several seconds.

"Capture it," said Yasmine, almost breathless, over the comms.

Mika's hard response held more vibrancy than it had earlier. "Destroy it."

Olivia, blinking as if her eyes were bothering her, circled the spectre with her gun drawn. "If you open the shield, even enough for a bullet, it might escape. You'll have to have a second shield ready."

I couldn't see the tire store beyond the lifted truck and wanted the quickest solution for us to continue before Cherney escaped too far. "Can I use your gun?"

She didn't hesitate, flipping the grip toward me.

The ammo would have mercury, silver, and more laced in it to deal with the denizens of Tarus. I checked the weapon, pressed the muzzle against my first shield, then formed a second as an oval bubble around me and the trapped spectre with a shape that pocketed my head, somewhat. If I failed, the shield would hold until the others arrived. I'd run out of air, if I weren't already dead. The memory of Olivia standing limp before the entity's touch flashed in my thoughts. It filled half my vision, an absence six inches from my face.

Here goes. Eyes locked on the void, I pierced a hole in the shield that trapped it and fired.

The cold touch against my fingers panicked my heart, but in that second the void dissolved, growing gray like the smoke from a rubbish pile, until it faded, leaving me to stare at the red of the truck. My ears rang, but the earbuds helped. I released both shields. The bullet clattered to the sidewalk, though I couldn't hear it.

"Let's go." I handed Olivia's weapon back to her and scrambled down the embankment to the parking lot.

The van sat nestled between the rear bumpers of two cars. A mechanic stood at the front of one, gaping in our direction.

I threw Haven against the van and found only our voyeur present. "Cherney's on foot." He hadn't moved uphill toward us. Even distracted with the spectre, we would have seen him.

Downhill, the open bays of a lube shop appeared quiet, but the gas station at the farther corner of the intersection had plenty of activity.

"He'll try to get a vehicle," Olivia suggested. As we started running down the slope, she alerted the others. "No sign of Cherney from our location, heading east to the intersection."

"Two locals within a minute of you. Sending them Cherney's description." Neddie sounded pleased.

My energy wasn't at its top, so the detection spell I threw into the bays of the oil change place was faint until we drew close in passing, then two figures glowed as they lounged unconcerned in the cool of the office.

I focused on the gas station with a gas-guzzling white classic and an odd little gray sedan. No one moved under the shade of the overhang.

We were running, both of our heads on swivels, when shouting came from the front of the convenience store where we couldn't see. Olivia, still with a bullet hole in her leg, kept up with me.

I didn't need Haven to find Cherney. As he fired a pistol into the chest of a large man, he held a young girl, six at the oldest, by her elbow while a frantic mother pleaded with him.

Olivia and I were five yards from the corner entrance to the convenience store, and he stood at the driver's door of an SUV another eight feet beyond that. He spotted us, casually aiming the muzzle toward the girl's temple. I couldn't see her face, but her shoulders heaved with sobbing.

I really want to kill you.

"Weapons on the ground," he said. Even as Olivia laid hers down, he fired at me; he missed, but caused me to dodge for cover behind a too-small concrete waste bin. "Get in and drive," he shouted at the mother.

His next shot caught Olivia in the stomach, still into the vest, but forcing her to bend and drop to one knee.

As I peeked at him edging for the rear door of the SUV behind the driver's side, he fired again. The mother wailed, but as she watched him move her daughter toward the vehicle, she opened the door.

He might kill them. Afterward.

I took a risk with my illusion; to Cherney, I appeared to

run for the back of the SUV, and if he fired, he might hit a gas pump and blow us all sky-high. From the garbage can, I didn't have a good angle on him, and I'd prefer his back to me.

It worked.

Cherney didn't fire, but he backed up, gun trained to the east where my illusion hid behind the SUV. "I'll kill her, I swear."

Quiet as a cat, I stood and took two steps, gaining a frantic glance from the mother. She didn't see the binding I threw, but the weapon in my hand caused her to gasp.

The spell slid off a binder's block, but I had already woven a lifting spell about his wrist and twisted.

I chose the arm he held the girl with, rather than the one that held the gun. With my focus locked on his head, I prowled forward while my illusory doppelganger stepped out from behind the back of the SUV.

While I wrenched Cherney's wrist and freed the girl, he began pumping shots into my illusion. I let it crumple to the ground. *Best he not fire into traffic.*

Controlling my clone, making it writhe, took more energy than I'd used in the last hour, but I played it well by waving my phantom gun about as if to get off a shot under his ceaseless barrage.

The girl dashed to the mother, who whisked her up, nearly bowling me over to escape.

I almost regretted it when his gun clicked empty. Only then did he turn toward the car and see me at the entrance to the store; he was peering down the barrel of my Glock. His eyes squinted as his fingers, those that had held the girl, lowered to his belt to tug out a clay coin.

Mika pulled up behind the SUV, driving a blue sedan that had grown pale and dull from the sun. There, my illusion faded into the tar. Lily sat in the passenger seat, watching as Mika cocked their head and studied me.

Cherney flipped his coin toward my chest with a thumbnail.

I held his eyes with mine, my jaw tight.

The curse bounced off my shield six inches from him, invisible to all but Mika and perhaps Lily.

He watched as the coin tumbled down to his feet. Time seemed to slow as the clay acted like an autumn leaf that floated and twisted to the ground. There it clattered, and a small piece chipped off the edge, a crescent that became visible for a moment before the green blasting spell tore into the asphalt and Cherney's knees.

More coins exploded at his waist and pockets, and a binding spell finally overcame his binder's block. There wasn't much of him left to hold.

I holstered my weapon and released the shield.

CHAPTER

THIRTY-ONE

As Mika opened their car door, I retreated to the glass window of the convenience store and leaned against it.

I drew in a deep breath, dragging in the stench of Cherney's viscera. Voices murmured from inside the store, but no one exited or approached us. He's dead. It didn't make me feel any better; Beth and Peter were still gone.

"You could have saved him." Mika threw an illusion over the remnants of the corpse, making it blurry and vaguely in the shape of an intact man.

Olivia opened the door of the convenience store. "FBI. Everyone move back from the entry. We'll need witness statements."

I couldn't restrain the start of a disturbed chuckle.

Lily had exited, studying me with Mika, so I nodded in response to the statement. I could have slipped a lifting spell around the shield and kept the coin from falling. It had crossed my mind.

"What will happen to the one we captured?" I asked.

Lily's eyes flicked to the window. "He will remain under *our* care."

Good. We had theories, in my old department, but no one really knew what happened to some we identified as threats to the Consociation. If I'd saved Cherney, he would have spent his life locked away. The families of the people he'd killed would have never had closure — or would they? "How will this all get explained?"

Mika tousled their pink hair and smoothed it back; they had a bruise across their jawline and new cuts from the last explosion. "Not our department, but usually something this massive gets split into little stories and the credit divided between the FBI and local enforcement."

I'd watch the headlines. *Maybe.* Fatigue draped over me like a weighted blanket.

Olivia exited the store and handed me a bottle of water. She hid her limp, but it was there.

As I drank, I spotted the mother and daughter watching from the soda station, their eyes wide and focused on me. *They saw two of me.* I emptied the bottle and turned to Mika, who had their phone out. "What will happen to the witnesses?"

Lily rubbed her lips and chin without looking my way while Mika lifted their head and caught my eyes. "It depends. Most we brush aside with excuses of panic-induced misunderstanding and counter-witnesses. Again, not our department."

"How about those who don't silence easily?" I asked.

"Yeah, those get more difficult." Mika gestured vaguely about the scene, including the asphalt where Cherney had emptied his weapon into my illusion. "The best we can do is try to keep the more unusual scenes from being public, but civilian safety comes first. You did well, Zach."

Olivia nodded, her eyes locked on me like an owl. "Will you be joining us?"

Mika returned to their phone. "He will."

I bristled at the assumption and opened my mouth. With a sharp inhale, I snapped my lips together, pursing them in frustration. I'd seen the damage that a few rogue Red Aegis could cause. The DRC, despite my mother's cautious concerns, served a valuable purpose. *Mika's right.* I pushed my ego down and answered Olivia. "Yes."

"That's my gym bro," said Dagen over the comms.

I snorted. "You okay, Dagen?"

"Pissed. Missed all the fun."

Mika held up their phone. "I've set the paperwork in motion. You've got this week to deal with personal matters, but I expect to see you on Monday morning. I'll have some papers for you to sign and your IDs. Once Everek gets here and gives you a look, we'll get you back to Phoenix."

A squad car pulled into the parking lot, lights flashing.

I began peeling myself out of the vest.

THIRTY-TWO

Late Wednesday night, I pulled my bike up to the bay that the band shared with the auto place. Redheaded William leaned beside the open door, smoking a joint.

One of my closest friends through college, he didn't bother offering more consolation as he'd already said his piece. "Glad you showed up," he said, voice tight from an inhale. He wore a black T-shirt with "People Not Prisons" emblazoned on the front, with gray cargos and purple Birkenstocks. Near my weight but shorter, he sported the extra around his waist.

"Yeah, me too." I'd vacillated for half the day, but my mind kept rolling back to the dead in Reno, including the one I'd killed. I didn't count Cherney; he had made his own choice.

"Stacey's running late. Seth's always late. You still planning on moving out?" He offered me a hit, but I waved it off as usual. "Apartments are expensive unless you're sharing the cost. Even then."

I stretched my hands up to the raised garage door,

staring in at our makeshift studio. Stacey's drum set took up half the space. Amps and stools dotted the remainder of the concrete floor. "I'm switching jobs." I'd never asked about the salary, but the Consociation paid well. "Just can't mope around that house."

"I get it. I do. New gig? Can you talk about it, or is it all hush-hush like the last one?"

More so. "I've just met them. I imagine it's the same." A hollow sensation filled my chest as silence crept in. Most practices, I'd have a story to tell about Peter or Beth. I didn't want to ask about his newest girlfriend.

William jerked his head back. "How'd you get scratched up?"

I still had leftovers from some of the heavier gashes left by the explosion. Everek had focused on the bruised ribs, swearing that they were the most difficult to heal. Through my curls, I rubbed the scar on my temple. "Work, mainly."

"Scrapping with the other data analysts?" He laughed. "Office artillery gone wrong. I want to see the video."

A smile tugged at my lips, and I let it form. "Not quite. But preferable." The banter felt good, even though I couldn't keep up my side. *Beats sitting in my thoughts.* "I wasn't going to come tonight. I'm glad I did."

"Me too." He nodded and scratched his head, then rubbed ash out of his short hair. He cut it to a short buzz. People sometimes thought he was military. *Far from it.*

"What are you working on?" I asked him.

"Gods. I'm all over the place. Mainly trying to keep the attention on deportation right now. People can't see it as bigotry unless you spell it out for them. The Immigration Advocates Network has been taking up a lot of my time. It's going to get bad. Worse." As William got into the meat of his work, I grabbed one of the stools and listened. The few times he'd gotten to speak with my dad, they'd locked onto each other.

The bay smelled like petroleum, always had, but it could be the fumes from the nearby shop. My guitar waited in the simple locker we kept on the side wall, but I resisted pulling it out. We had the whole night.

"I got tomorrow off," William said.

I frowned, unsure if I'd missed some comment or thread. "Tomorrow?"

"Yeah, for the funerals."

"Yes, the funerals." My stomach twisted. "Tomorrow."

CHAPTER

THIRTY-THREE

I stood beside my mom, listening to the conversation with Peter's parents. My eyes ached from tears, and theirs were redder, while my gaze trailed through the crowd to the flower-laden caskets, closed and sealed. *Shredded*. The funeral home director had been clear that little could be done to make them viewable. Nausea rose.

A figure sharpened in my unfocused gaze as my brother John walked along the rows toward me. As always, an easy smile spread across his face, though I could see pain, perhaps mine reflected. "Air?" he asked.

In my periphery, I saw our mother, Samantha, flick a glance at us, but she kept Peter's parents engaged. I let John grab the elbow of my suit and pivot us toward the front entrance of the funeral home. Friends and family of Peter and Beth crowded the open entry, snatching quick looks at me. Some I knew, even mutual friends we'd gone dancing with, but most had already said their condolences, and I wasn't in my best form.

John held the door, letting the dry air bake us. "You holding up?"

My younger brother had the same tight black curls I had, but a rounder face, less height, and more tats. The oil from his mechanic's job stained his calloused fingers. As we stepped into the shade of the overhang, he put his hand on the back of my neck. The scent of cigarettes wafted from a pair of Beth's relatives.

"As good as it gets." I took a deep breath of the baked air, easing the churning in the pit of my stomach.

"You didn't return my call last night." His words weren't a judgment or condemnation; he just probed.

"I was practicing with the band."

His smile brightened. "Good. All good." We moved to the edge of the shade with the traffic on the road in our view. "Mom says you're trying to get yourself killed."

I noted his smirk and forced a weak smile in return. "Yeah. I'm moving to a new department."

"Oh, that one." We all knew Mom's warnings about the DRC. "So maybe she's right."

"No." I tugged at the collar of my suit jacket. "I need a more active role. There's so much going on. People getting hurt."

"Well, vigilante is better than self-destruction. Try not to get hurt." He raised an eyebrow at the scar on my temple. "Oops, too late. Let me revise. Try not to get yourself killed."

We stood for a moment, cars drifting by, before I mentioned our sister. "Yvette looks good. About the same."

"Yeah, self-absorbed. Nice she flew out. She's booked on a flight tonight."

"We talked. She suggested I get a dog."

John guffawed a bit too loudly. "Shit. Sorry." He turned to check the smokers. "Quite a turnout. Haven't seen Izzie in a while. Nice that she came out."

"Barking up the wrong tree, brother." He'd always taken notice of her.

"So you've said. I'm just mentioning that it was nice of her to come out."

"Angel too." I gave him a sideways glance.

"Yeah, Angel too." John cleared his throat. "Head back in? You don't look as pale as you did."

"Thanks." As we headed for the door, my cell buzzed, so I checked it while we were still outside.

Mika texted, WOULD YOU MIND IF WE STOPPED IN TO PAY OUR RESPECTS?

I paused, not because I'd mind, but over the formal way they'd asked. NOT AT ALL. THANK YOU.

John waited, not asking, but obviously curious.

With a shrug, I raised the phone. "My new workmates wanting to drop by."

"Nice of them." He opened the door for me.

Anne and my mom hovered in the entry and moved in on us as we entered. My mother had her wavy black hair down on her shoulders and wore more jewelry than usual. Her black dress suit contrasted with Anne's calf-length skirt and heels, according to their natures.

"One of Beth's friends, Lacy, wants to read a poem. Will it be appropriate?" Mom asked me.

Anne watched with matching intent. "Or not inappropriate, at least." She had Beth's brown hair, but had styled it in curls for the funeral.

I forced a comforting smile. "Lacey's favorite poet is Emily Dickinson, not Keats." At their blank gazes, I added, "It'll be fine."

Mom sniffed. "We'll be starting. You should work your way to the front."

The last place I wanted to be was at the caskets, but I nodded. I'd come early to touch the wood and flowers, and to cry. With them leading the way, John escorted me through the faces. William, Seth, Angel, and Izzie were among them. My sister, Yvette, sat in the second row alone. Dad was having an intense conversation with a man I didn't know.

The scent of lilies met me as John and I took seats. The caskets lay like ponderous blocks on the tables with polished sides and gleaming metal. Beth and Peter would be cremated; their parents had agreed to their wishes. Ever the lawyer, Beth had put it in writing. My tears started again.

I'm going to miss you.

John put his arm over my shoulders, casually watching the crowd on the other side of the room.

I rubbed my stubble, then my eyes, turning when my mother used her sharp voice for my dad, corralling him away from his conversation.

A flash of pink caught my eye, and I twisted to find Mika taking a seat in the back. Dagen waved. Olivia just stared. The suits they wore might have been their work clothes for the cut, but in better shape than the last time I saw them.

With a sigh, I turned to the front, ready to say goodbye.

THIRTY-FOUR

When I stepped into the FBI building just before 8 a.m. on Monday morning, Mika was talking to the guard there. "Newbie's here. Gotta go. Let me know what you think of the book."

I approached, helmet in hand, wearing a suit that I assumed met their business attire standards. The tie had been a deal-breaker, and I'd said as much yesterday when we'd talked. "Am I early, or late?"

Mika gestured for me to follow. "On time. Until we have a case, everyone's on time."

"And when we have a case?" The shoes I wore clacked on the floor, only one of the many reasons I preferred sneakers.

"You saw; we're often late. Did you get a run in this morning?"

"I did." *Why?* I'd gotten used to Mika's style leading with a game of questions. Their personality when on a job seemed different from other times, or perhaps it mattered which side of the investigation you were on; I couldn't tell. *Yet.*

"Good."

We reached the door to the DRC, and I broke down and asked, "Why?"

"Better." Mika led the way into the small hall. "I need to know you're back on your schedule, not falling apart over all this. You've lost your closest people, and killed at least one man, depending on how you look at it."

My voice echoed in the confines. "Cherney deserved it. His choice."

"Mostly." Mika opened the door leading to the main office.

Olivia sat at a desk in the corner to my left, swiveling to face us as we entered. Neddie leaned over a station. *Phistrel's, now mine.* I placed my helmet and water bottle on the conference table, waiting for direction.

"Grab a chair, Zach. You're mine for a couple of hours." Neddie didn't turn as she spoke, but she took a seat at the computer beside Olivia.

I moved to take the empty chair on the other side of Neddie, but she jabbed a thumb over her shoulder. "Not Dagen's. Grab one from the conference table."

"Okay." I took one, moving to her right elbow. "What are we doing?"

"Training on the systems. There's some similarity to your last job, but some other tools available. Sit. Listen."

I complied, and we spent over an hour before Dagen arrived. For a split second, I saw a glimmer of the werewolf I'd met the first time in the room, the day Peter and Beth had been murdered. Then she smiled and headed for her desk, smacking the back of my head as she passed behind.

"What's that for?"

"Not being Phistrel. You'll get used to it."

I doubt I will. "Not my fault."

"Sure it is. If you'd been a colossal screwup, then you wouldn't be here." She slouched in her chair, feet kicked out. Her grin widened as she logged onto her computer. "I had hopes."

It took four full hours for Neddie to walk me through the system, including prepping a report that I'd have to fill out for the Cherney incident. Yasmine had come in near the end and sat with Mika at the conference table engaged in a lively conversation.

When Neddie stood up to pronounce that I'd adequately completed her orientation, I thanked her and returned my chair to the table. I still felt a little stiff around the team. Olivia had remained busy the entire time, reading reports. Dagen had been the only one to interject a snarky comment or three.

Mika rose as I turned to head for my workstation and the lengthy report that I needed to complete. "Olivia's driving."

I paused, waiting for more before finally asking, "Where?"

"Lookout Tavern. Do you know the place?"

"Yeah . . ." I stretched the word out, unsure why we'd be heading there in the middle of the day.

Yasmine sprang for the door. "I'll grab my bag."

Dagen appeared beside me, slapping my back with a glimpse of gray Ya-Keya. "Liquid lunch. Mika needs to get you drunk."

Needs? My confused expression turned to a wince. "I'm not much of a drinker. Not during the day. A little on the weekends."

Mika cocked their head. "We've been through hell last week. I'd like us to loosen up a little and get to know each other. You don't have to drink; Olivia doesn't."

Neddie followed Yasmine out the door. "Have fun, kids. I've got work to do."

I studied Mika, then Olivia and Dagen. *It* had *been hell, from the start.* "Okay, I'm in." I held up a finger. "On one condition."

Mika's eyebrow raised. "What's that?"

"I pick the music."

AFTERWORD

Review here - https://www.amazon.com/review/create-review/?&asin=B0FH5J4XL2 or the book's page.

A quick thanks and a hope that you enjoyed this story, if you did then a review is always helpful.

I've got plans for Zach out west, next will be a dip in the Pacific. I'm loving the team dynamics, and I need to get him settled into a new life, without Beth and Peter.

CONSOCIATION RECORDS

Demon - Western Nomenclature

Origin: Tarus Realm
Rated as highly dangerous.

Physical appearances, while primarily gaseous, vary widely, though tend to mimic summoner, with myriad adjustments. Variance to appearances Seem designed to inspire primal fear incorporating fangs, teeth, horns, and claws, or distorted forms. In cases of possession, only Dragon-shifters are capable of clearly identifying demon entities within a host.
Demon attacks can be physical and emotional depending upon their nature. Approximately 85% appear to feed and pursue heightened emotions such as panic or rage. Possession is possible, but coercion is more likely. It is unknown if possession is a universal capability, or limited to specific entities.
Their entry into adjacent realms can be through direct summoning or opportunity if a portal is created. Reports from travels inside of Tarus detail a wide variety of demon forms.
Methods of expelling from realms include iron, salt, and ammonia. While Dragon-shifters have alternative methods, the exact methodology is

Dragon-shifter - Western Nomenclature

Origin: Salmhalla Realm

Physical appearances in the Earth Realm are designed to appear fully humanoid, though that is only a portion of their form, while some remnant remains in Salmhalla. Dragon-shifters have been known to utilize claws and tails that they bring through the ever-present portal between realms that surrounds their person.
Since their return from their self-imposed expulsion from the other realms, they have confined their activities to the Consociation and refuse to divulge any more magical knowledge. Their stated objective is to protect the Consociation members from the harm they caused by sharing information to Humans which bred the creation of witches, arcanists, Werewolves, and Vampires.
Contact with the Salmhalla Realm is forbidden and has been met with deadly force on many occasions.
Within the Consociation, they promote the absolute restriction on interaction with the Tarus Realm and support the departments with any enforcement to that effort. In this, they utilize

Draugr / Draughr - Western Nomenclature

Origin: Tarus Realm
Rated as highly dangerous.

Draugrs present as humanoid on the Earth Realm with skeletal remains indistinguishable from Humans. Primary visible differences include the lack of skin or eyes, teeth more appropriate to a carnivore, and misaligned muscle distribution. Internally, most organs are replicated but vestigial, with an emphasis on digestion that defies scientific explanation, though many hypotheses exist. Their speed and strength exceeds those of Humans by a significant margin.
Their entry into adjacent realms can be through direct summoning or opportunity if a portal is created. Once introduced into an environment, they can become fiercely territorial. They have been known to survive for extensive periods of time without any sustenance; documented trials have been extensive.
Their physique remains constant in Tarus, based on multiple reports, though no scientific autopsies have been performed.
Draugrs can be destroyed through

Dur-Alf - Indigenous Nomenclature

Visible indications: dark-green color;
crumbling, dusty texture
Status: Prohibited
Classification: Planet realm

The fourth of eight known planets,
Dur-Alf orbits a G2V star and has no
known satellites of its own. Polar caps
are extensive. Large bodies of water
are landlocked in the north and south
with a belt of deserts and jungles
around the equator. An abundance of
rivers, lakes, and forests support a
wide variety of life. An axial tilt
of less than 20% causes mild seasonal
variation.
Dwarves are the dominant sentient
species on the planet. Little is known
of their societies or cultures, though
some mention of warlike activities
have been reported by reliable
sources. Their generally isolationist
nature limits direct observation,
and those who do frequent the Earth
Realm are notoriously reticent. Their
relationship with the Kuru Kuru is
unknown, though there appears to be
no animosity. The hypothesis of other
sentient species has yet to have any
viable confirmation and primarily

Dwarf – Western Nomenclature

Origin: Dur-Alf Realm
Rated as potentially dangerous.

Short in comparison to Human stature,
some Dwarves have been reported up
to five feet tall, though they range
closer to four feet on average.
Facial hair presents on the species
as a whole and holds some cultural
significance that can only be
hypothesized. Lipofuscin pigment
in the iris, along with Rayleigh
scattering and low melanin content
lead to a wide variety of eye colors,
including purple and red. Internal
organs are comparable to the family
Usidae, with some deviations.
Dwarven perception of the realms is
inherent, with two mentions of rare
anomalies in their species of those
who cannot interact. Their interaction
with Earth has been ongoing long before
Dragon-shifters spread the knowledge
to Humans. Proficient in many areas
of martial combat, some have quickly
embraced modern weaponry developed by
Humans. Relations over the centuries
have been strained with Humans,
primarily over the introduction of
Werewolves and Vampires; the creation
of the Consociation caused further

Ghoul - Western Nomenclature

Origin: Tarus Realm
Rated as dangerous.

A mindless scavenger, the Ghoul contains the same symbiote that a Vampire does. This revelation, in conjunction with existing stigma, complicated Vampire-Human relations. Ghouls present as humanoid but hairless with gray skin, black claws akin to a bear's, carnivorous teeth, and black eyes.
They will survive on dead flesh, but quickly attack the living for sustenance, and can be starved to death over periods of captivity. Autopsies have revealed a closed digestive system with an enlarged stomach. Other organs, most similar to Earth animals, are shriveled and atrophied, including the brain. It is hypothesized that the symbiotes control the actions as some group mind. These views exacerbated the difficulty in relations with the Vampires.
Methods of destruction or expelling from realms include iron, salt, and ammonia, but they can be surprisingly resilient. Most witches rely on crushing spells, followed by fire. Dragon-shifters have been known to

Haven - Western Nomenclature

Visible indications: thick white mist

Classification: Planar realm

Vastly unexplored except by the Merfolk, little has been identified of Haven. Apparently uninhabited, the realm offers no gravity, land, or anything more substantial than fog. The air is breathable and the rolling mist contains water. Light is ambient with no discernible source.
Human witches have explored the realm and identified bordering realms outside of Salmhalla and Tarus, with some disastrous losses.
The Dragon-shifters are reticent in discussion of the realm, but the Consociation only offers warnings on the danger of bordering realms; no prohibitions exist.
Pre-Akkadian legends speak of superior spells available through the Haven Realm, but experimentation has not yielded any new results above those already known. Merfolk, Dragon-shifters, and Dwarves have not aided in this research, and no reports exist of their usage of the Haven Realm outside of expectations.

Jinn – Western Nomenclature

Origin: Tarus Realm
Rated as highly dangerous.

A disputed entity, misclassed as a
Demon, the Jinn has the same physical
appearances, primarily gaseous, which
vary widely, though tend to mimic
summoner. Like the Demon, variances to
appearances appear designed to inspire
primal fear incorporating fangs, teeth,
horns, and claws, or distorted forms.
No definitative case of possession is
tied to these cryptids.
The defining aspects of the Jinn is
their trickery and reliance on coercion
and attacks that utilize inciting
others. Considered more clever than
Demons, they still appear to feed and
pursue heightened emotions such as
panic or rage.
Their entry into adjacent realms can be
through direct summoning or opportunity
if a portal is created. No reports of a
sighting of Jinn inside Tarus exists,
but they might have been identified as
Demons, be exteremely rare, or their
ability to avoid detection is skilfull.
Ongoing attempts at classification
continue.
Methods of expelling from realms
include iron, salt, and ammonia. While

Kuru Kuru - Indigenous Nomenclature

Origin: Dur-Alf Realm
Rated as non-dangerous.

Short in comparison to Human stature,
there are only two sources which offer
limited descriptions. Cloaked in each
instance, both describe a flattened
muzzle, but diverge over whether the
skin is covered with fur or feathers.
Since joining Consociation efforts,
reports exist mentioning brief
sightings of their brown cloaks, but
no trace evidence has ever been left
behind.
Their recent inauguration into
the Consociation was facilitated
by Dragon-shifters with no direct
interaction during sessions, but no
contestation by the Dwarves. Human and
Mer delegations did offer preliminary
concerns at not being able to interview
the Kuru Kuru directly, but set aside
their stance at the request of the
Dragon-shifters and Dwarves.
At the onset, they offered their
services to the Consociation and have
performed with consistent efficiency.
Considering their ability to remain
hidden, a wide array of hypotheses
exists over their magical abilities

Lich - Western Nomenclature

Origin: Tarus Realm
Rated as extremely dangerous.

A lich is created by a willful witch
who enters the Tarus Realm and commits
a forbidden ritual using the Haven and
Tarus Realms. The details have been
purged by the Consociation, and the
rare sightings are attributed to acts
in the past, rather than present.
Those few encountered have presented
as skeletal, often with remnants of
jewelry, armor, clothing, and even
weapons.
Undead, like Vampires and many denizens
of the Tarus Realm, a Lich requires no
sustenance. In time, the body decays
off the bones and the form is held by
spirit and Earth Realm magic. Often
seeming intelligent, the rare Lich that
has been loosed on Earth maintains
devastating control over the realms.
It is theorized that their long time in
the Tarus Realm aids in their growing
mastery over adjacent realms; Earth,
Haven, and Ya Keya. Levitation and
keen eyeless sight are attributed to
this practice. While intelligent and
cunning, they lack any discernable
motive or purpose except a propensity
to destroy and kill.

Mer - Western Nomenclature
Ishi-Iyai-Eyai-I - Indigenous Nomenclature

Visible indications: blue-green color; liquid texture
Status: Prohibited
Classification: Planet realm

The third planet orbiting an unclassified but reportedly hotter star, Mer is defined as a water planet with a single satellite. No other defined characteristics have been offered or answered regarding the planet. Merfolk claim to be the single sentient lifeform on Mer. Along with unknown species, dolphins, porpoises, and whales have been transplanted to the realm centuries before the formation of the Consociation.
No reported Human expeditions to the Mer Realm have survived to offer firsthand observations, though many were organized prior to the prohibition. The Merfolk joined the Consociation in part to document their refusal to allow access to their realm by any of the Consociation member species.
Prior to Merfolk appearance at the Consociation, most hypotheses defined the realm as planar.
Only Dragon-shifter and Dwarven

Merfolk / Mer - Western Nomenclature

Origin: Mer Realm
Rated as non-dangerous.

Their natural or typical biology is unknown and undisclosed, though they are hypothesized to be a form of sea mammal. Interrealm movement allows the Merfolk to transmogrify into mammalian or Dwarven biology, indistinguishable from native physiology. They predominantly present as nonbinary on the Earth realm.
At some point prior to the Akkadian wars, most Merfolk stopped inhabiting Earth's seas, though they reportedly continued their relations with the Dwarves.
Their return to Earth to support the Consociation, at the urging of the Dwarves, came with a requirement that prohibited Humans from attempting to enter the Mer Realm. In return, they brought extensive research of the Ya Keya and Tarus Realms to the Consociation, and an agreement to divulge all future investigation of those realms and their inhabitants. Merfolk are innately connected to the realms and can be proficient practitioners, to the extent that many

Revenant - Western Nomenclature

Origin: Tarus Realm
Rated as dangerous.

Incorporeal in the Earth Realm, they
present as a vaguely bipedal shadow.
In this form, they present no danger
to anyone except to the weakened
such as the comatose or those near to
death. They will possess the weak,
but based on their habits, prefer
to inhabit fresh corpses. In Tarus,
they are harmless to the healthy, and
indistinguishable from shadows.
Their entry into adjacent realms can be
through direct summoning or opportunity
if a portal is created. Their potential
for danger is contingent on their
host body. Control can vary based
on their experience with animating
that type of physique. They typically
avoid confrontation where possible
and have been known to exist for
extended periods in remote or abandoned
locations, possibly moving from one
host to another.
Methods of expelling from realms
include iron, salt, and ammonia,
but they can be elusive in their
incorporeal form. Dragon-shifters
have more direct methods, unavailable
and unknown to Human practitioners.

Salmhalla - Western Nomenclature

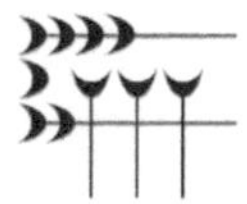

Visible indications: metallic gold color; liquid texture
Status: Prohibited
Classification: Planar realm

According to unconfirmed records dating back prior to the Akkadian wars, the Salmhalla Realm is a plane of ambient sunlight, breathable air, and hot temperatures. The terrain includes dominating mountains and grassy hills, with rare mentions of various other biomes. The wildlife and plants detailed vary between those on Earth and stranger depictions that align with many mythical cryptids. Dragon-shifters have confirmed that many varieties of felines have been transplanted to the Salmhalla Realm, beyond that, they offer no responses as to the nature of the plane. Their refusal to allow Human interaction with their plane is enforced with a fervor that has led to death, disappearance, mental illness, and loss of memory. Stated reasoning always includes an apology for their previous interference with Human development by their gifting of

Spectre / Specter / Banshee – Western Nomenclature

Origin: Tarus Realm
Rated as extremely dangerous.

Incorporeal, little is known of these rare denizens of the Tarus Realm. They present as any shape to serve their purpose, and move through matter like liquid through a porous stone. Light does not reflect or penetrate their surface, resulting in a void easily recognizable in bright conditions, and hazardous in dark. Their contact with corporeal beings can result in rotting flesh, death, and varying degrees of insanity. Despite well-documented reports, analysis has not determined their motives or set patterns. Flight and report is the recommended action when confronted with these entities.
Mercury and iron have proved effective at expelling them back to the Tarus Realm.
Do not attempt bindings.
Two occasions of encapsulating shields have proven to hold them, though the durations were short and this method is untested in a controlled environment.
Dragon-shifters can expel them, and are best equipped to deal with Spectres.

Tarus - Western Nomenclature

Visible indications: dark-gray color;
cloudy texture
Status: Prohibited
Classification: Planar realm

The plane has no ambient light in a
spectrum visible to the Human eye.
Other species report infrared light
spectrums at least in the IR-A range.
Tests confirm oxygen-rich air with
negligible humidity. No sources of
water have ever been catalogued in
the rocky terrain.
Merfolk expeditions provide the bulk
of Consociation documentation but
occasional corroborating reports have
come from those who have survived
unintended forays into the realm. It
is hypothesized that an expertise with
the Haven Realm provides protection.
Predominant species identified include
demons, ghouls, draugrs, and revenants,
though most of the data is based on
cryptid activity at portals, not from
any census taken during explorations.
These species also prove to be the
most active within the realm and in
proximity to portals, so disputes
exist over the data. Rarely seen or
infrequent denizens include spectres,

Vampire - Western Nomenclature

Joining into a commensal symbiotic relationship with a fungal-like organism native to Tarus, Humans transform their biology radically and permanently. Prolonged exposure to the realm can cause the symbiosis, as can blood-to-blood contamination with a Vampire. Exact periods of times, or volumes cannot be established and some Humans appear immune.
The resulting mutation offers the recipient enhanced cellular regrowth that coincides with the Vampire able to change physical attributes and extend their lifespan. Strength and speed are increased in degrees that vary from one individual to the next. Resistance to disease, infection, and toxins are linked to the primary reported cause for seeking this mutation, fatal conditions can be reversed.
Adverse conditions include sterility, the re-engineered metabolism requirement for red blood cells, and cellular weakness to radiation. Transition metals, in varying degrees depending on the element, can disrupt cells.
In present day, the stigma over Vampires has lessened through

Werewolf - Western Nomenclature
Hunter / Dreamer
Indigenous
Nomenclature

The connection between the Ya Keya
Realm and indoctrination of a Human
into a Werewolf is only partially
codified. While a witch is in contact
with the Ya Keya Realm, or substantial
bodily fluids of a Werewolf, cells
are altered. The resulting mutation
creates a persistent tether to the Ya
Keya Realm. In Human form, the immune
system is enhanced to near Vampiric
levels, appetite is increased, and
senses are more acute.
Through transmogrification, Werewolves
can increase muscle mass directly from
the Ya Keya realm, though the dynamics
have not been codified. Muscles, hair,
bones, teeth, and claws can be shifted
toward their full bipedal canine form
in any varying degree. Those born
from a Werewolf, or Werewolves, have
increased control over this partial
state and tend to have extended
lifespans.
Adverse conditions include sensitivity
to some Earth plants and aggressive
tendencies in an altered state. The
ability to manipulate other realms is
lost without arcane methods.
Metals damage cells with prolonged

Ya Keya – Historical Nomenclature

Visible indications: light gray color;
mist texture
Status: Prohibited
Classification: Planar realm

Historically identified as the
hunter's dream world, it the first
interaction between Humans and the
realms, dating before contact with
the Dragon-shifters.
Because Merfolk have the same
susceptibility to cellular mutation
from contact with the realm, few
expeditions have returned with
comprehensive details. Technology has
proved ineffective as portals close
without contact so drones were lost,
and contamination suits did not stop
cellular mutation.
The temperate plane contains a variety
of Earthlike terrains such as forests,
plains, and savannahs lit with a
blue-gray twilight. Rivers and ponds
were noted, but no larger bodies of
water. Clouds were present, with one
report of fog.
Wildlife sightings were numerous, if
brief, and depictions mimicked Earth
herbivorous prey such as rabbit, deer,

ACKNOWLEDGMENTS

April keeps me on track, after having to listen to hours of planning and plotting. She follows behind with the proof to fix the broken parts.

Robyn Huss, my editor, has been with me since the first series.

The Fireside Group; Billy, Siena, Rosemary, Mark, Tim, Vail, and Katharine keep me challenged to do better. Arrash and Michele from Jody Lynn Nye's DragonCon workshop keep me on task with the most intricate details and loving support. Dianne and Brett from Apex have been there for me.

Jody Lynn Nye's workshop will always be my go to suggestion for an in-person critique for any aspiring writers. Her insight is invaluable.

I still miss David Farland's gentle mentorship. Please pick up one of his books and enjoy the magic he endowed upon the world. Writers, study his lessons at Apex Writers.

Thank you.

www.ingramcontent.com/pod-product-compliance
Lightning Source LLC
Chambersburg PA
CBHW061227310726
48971CB00007B/1967